T0050539

Mad Gods
& Englishmen

A Fantasy

Mad Gods & Englishmen

A Fantasy

Ian Armer

Winchester, UK
Washington, USA

First published by Roundfire Books, 2013
Roundfire Books is an imprint of John Hunt Publishing Ltd., Laurel House, Station Approach,
Alresford, Hants, SO24 9JH, UK
office1@jhpbooks.net
www.johnhuntpublishing.com
www.roundfire-books.com

For distributor details and how to order please visit the 'Ordering' section on our website.

Text copyright: Ian Armer 2012

ISBN: 978 1 84694 953 1

All rights reserved. Except for brief quotations in critical articles or reviews, no part of this
book may be reproduced in any manner without prior written permission from the publishers.

The rights of Ian Armer as author have been asserted in accordance with the Copyright, Designs
and Patents Act 1988.

A CIP catalogue record for this book is available from the British Library.

Design: Stuart Davies

Printed and bound by CPI Group (UK) Ltd, Croydon, CR0 4YY

We operate a distinctive and ethical publishing philosophy in all
areas of our business, from our global network of authors to
production and worldwide distribution.

For Jessica

It is better to follow no saint than six.

Indian Proverb

Foreword

by Anthony Peake

Hollywood. The very name evokes images of sun-drenched vistas, beautiful people in open-top cars cruising down the wide, palm lined streets, of movie stars and fortunes being made behind every shiny façade; a place where dreams come true. However this is a facsimile, a simulacrum as French philosopher Jean Baudrillard would term it. The real Hollywood is found in the run-down bars and the flop houses frequented by those that the American Dream has passed by on its way down Sunset Boulevard. For these individuals Hollywood is a hard, stark place where survival depends upon quick wits, and even quicker fists. This is the Hollywood of James Ellroy, Horace McCoy, Steve Fisher and Charles Bukowski. These writers knew the real Hollywood because they experienced it first-hand. In their novels they used the dialogue of the gutter to explain the inner-life of their characters, words that accurately reflected the sordid world they describe. Not for them the slick witticisms of the screenwriters but more the blunt power of an expletive-ridden eruption of bile and venom.

That Hollywood consists of a world superimposed upon another world is central to Ian Armer's debut novel, *Mad Gods and Englishmen*. His central character, private detective Tommy Storm, is one of the under-achievers surviving on his wits and little else in this unforgiving environment. He drinks too much, treats women as simple gratification devices, and is well on the road to his own personal hell. However the Hollywood created by Armer is more than simply another re-tread of the classic noir detective fiction. This is a world where reality starts to blur at the edges and another, hidden, universe begins to appear. Soon the two superimposed worlds of Hollywood are being invaded by another world, a world more real than the simulacra and simulation that we all take for granted.

By cleverly embroidering into his plot a fascinating and bizarre situation called "Double You Day" – shortened to "W-Day" – Armer moves a seemingly clichéd "gumshoe" plot into something far stranger, and far more philosophically challenging. The classic storyline of the search for a missing person turns into a battle for the soul of humanity and takes us into the realm of the Demiurge and first century Gnostic theology. We have now moved from the safe, predictable world of Cornell Woolrich and Elmore Leonard into an anti-universe of Jorge Borges, William Blake and Philip K Dick.

This book is a classic of its kind. It has to be read at least twice in order to not only appreciate how Armer cleverly has his characters' personalities reflect Gnostic concepts of universal duality and the illusory nature of reality itself but also how he places subtle, and some not-so-subtle references to the master of all speculative fiction, Philip K Dick.

Anthony Peake is author of several bestselling books, including *The Daemon* and *The Labyrinth of Time: The Illusion of Past, Present and Future*.

PART ONE

Chapter 1

My fall had been planned from the start; an amusing distraction of exiled and vainglorious Lucifer. Malicious and venal, crowned in deceit and robed with a shock crimson hue of back-stabbing genius. And in believing I was smart enough to evade such criminal treachery, I presumed the slow descent down the straight razor's edge of truth was for those of a weaker disposition. Come the worst, some twist of fate or stroke of luck would redeem my tattered soul.

The plan set in motion against me, as I can best reckon it, began that cool March afternoon in Hollywood, the perfect home for the unassuming lull of such insidious corruption I'd grown used to.

I had been sitting in Mr Woo's Chinese restaurant for three hours, drinking beer and aiming for the bulls-eye of killing both time and my liver, schlepping down his despicable noodles and listening to the old bastard's unwanted opinions. I hated the son-of-a-bitch but the beer was cheap and I had a hard-on for Woo's granddaughter, Chi, sadly absent as I hung upon my own arrival, cursing my position in life and all about this rotten, no-good world.

'I don't like you drunk, Tommy,' said Woo, wiping down the table next to mine. 'You're rude to the other diners and you're rude to me. It shows a distinct lack of class.'

'Class,' I responded flatly, swigging from the bottle. 'Besides, I'm not drunk. Give me another beer.'

'No way, Tommy, you've had enough. Go home. Sleep it off.'

'At least let me finish my noodles, for Christ's sake! I paid for the bastards. I also paid for the beers in case it slipped your mind. Nobody forced you to take my hard-earned money and put a beer in my hand, did they?' I shouted.

'Hard-earned,' snorted Woo. 'Don't make me laugh, Tommy!

When was the last time you actually worked?'

'As a matter of fact, I'm on a case right now! I'm meeting myself here in about five minutes!'

'No, *you* Tommy, not the twin,' said Woo, moving onto another table to kill germs with his dirty rag and spittle. 'I mean, look at you! It's like your twin got the best and left the shit behind! How can the same person be so different?'

Woo had a point. The memory of that bright, February morning, as sharp as a cut, had never been settled in my mind. How long had it been? Three years, already? Three years since waking up in the apartment and seeing myself shaving at the sink through the open bathroom door. They'd nicknamed it 'W-Day' (short for 'Double-You Day') at the time, a moment when thousands of people across the world suddenly manifested their own 'twin'.

I could hear my voice slowly reason out what had happened back then and remember that I – *that is to say, my twin* – was surprisingly calm and good natured about the whole affair, cheerily breezing through the mind-warping turmoil of that day's events.

And now, as Woo cleaned tables whistling show tunes with a tuneless gait, the door to the restaurant opened and in I strode; clean shaven, smartly attired and every inch the professional. God, I made myself sick. I scratched my week-old stubble as I watched Woo fawn over me like a lover, complimenting me on the new shirt and haircut and then offering to buy me a drink on the house, the wrinkly little ass-kisser.

'Take a seat, Mr Storm,' gestured Woo. 'What about that drink?'

'Just a sparkling water, please,' I courteously replied.

'You want ice and lemon with that?'

'Please,' I said, following up with a winning flash of pearly white teeth as Woo scuttled off, eagerly fixing the drink as if on a promise.

'Christ!' I muttered, idly picking at the noodles before taking another swig of beer. If there was any justice, Woo would be kissing my ass and casually offering up his female staff for my sinister amusement.

'You're drunk,' I noted, casting an eye over the collection of bottles the management refused to clear in order to shame me.

'Yeah,' I answered quietly. 'So, what gives?'

'We got another reminder about the rent.'

'Ah, screw the rent. What else?'

'We got a case.'

My interest piqued. 'What is it?'

I reached across and pinched a noodle, swallowing it down. 'You ever heard of Anthony Prendergast?'

I shook my head. I continued.

'He's a big-shot film producer. Makes crap that all the critics hate but Joe Public adore. Remember that flick about the gay emasculated Jewish Toreador: *Horns of Desire?*'

Once again I shook my head.

'One critic kindly described it as…wait a second, let me get this right.' I pulled out a scrap of paper upon which I had quoted the review verbatim. 'Here we are; *Horns of Desire is a nonsensical exercise in cheap manipulation and gaping plot holes. Producer Anthony Prendergast's multi-million dollar grand folly is the cinematic equivalent of somebody pissing in your face for three consecutive hours.'* I folded away the paper. 'That's one of the better reviews. And yet the film grossed its budget back five times over during its run in theatres.'

'Fascinating,' I replied. 'What's the case?'

'His daughter, all of twenty-one, has eloped.'

'Eloped? Do people still do that?'

'Prendergast suspects that she's run off with the very-married leading man of his new flick.'

'Who is?'

'I can't say.'

'Can't or won't?'

I watched myself lean back into the chair with a weary sigh. 'Tommy, choose either option, but if you think I'm going to tell you, so when pissed you can shoot your mouth off to all and sundry, think again. This case requires tact. Any scandal involving his main lead will affect the box office of his new film. It's a delicate case with a respectable client who's paying well in excess of what we normally charge. This could really turn things around for us and I can't afford you screwing it up, especially with Jake breathing down our neck for his rent money! Just let me handle this one, okay?'

'Jesus Christ!' I yelled, my temper suddenly flaring. 'So it finally comes to this? You take over, muscle me out and leave me to scrounge like a rat in trash? Well, *fuck you!*'

'Are you even listening to me, Tommy? Let me spell it out; you drink too much, okay? And when you drink it brings out the worst in you. You act without thinking and I suffer the consequences! And as for your mouth! God, I've seen you spit knives in conversation when drunk!'

'You bastard,' I growled, banging my fist on the table and toppling the line of bottles.

Woo finally returned with the sparkling water, placing it before me with a knock-toothed smile before turning my way, collecting the fallen bottles and saying, 'Tommy, get out of here, okay?'

I grabbed my jacket off the back of the chair, fitted the faithful brown and battered Berkeley hat upon my head and left without a word.

Stepping out into the blaze of the L.A. sun, I figured I should nail Chi just to get back at Woo. Maybe get her pregnant and have Woo babysit our mixed-race bastard as I tried for more in the room next door. And I'd ensure that two-faced, noodle-loving *gonif* would hear every vile, nightmarish deed and twisted violation I could magic up from inside my trousers.

As I walked on the fantasy grew stale. All I really wanted was another drink. My guts squirmed under the intense heat of that burning desire. And as I traipsed along, scuffing my shoes and doddering about the sidewalk, trying to keep it together, I began to think more on what Woo had said: *how can the same person be so different?*

Amid the thick-set confusion and horror of those weeks and months after W-Day, many of the 'originals' had set about their twins. Many were killed in a panic, a good number carefully knocked-off for various reasons. A man in Boston was killed by his "twin" after returning home and discovering him in bed with his wife. It later emerged that the manifest twin had already plotted with the wife to kill the original husband who had been physically abusing her for a number of years. It was a golden opportunity in a moment of passion.

A fact that always struck me concerned the twin; it transpired he had no such violent urges to abuse the wife, nor did he drink or smoke - a similar trait of all twins. It appeared they always got a clean slate. As if a lifetime of accumulated Karma, bad deeds, vice and obscenity was left behind in the original model. It seemed grossly unfair, as if the good wheat had been separated from the chaff *but* – as the Boston case proved – they were more than capable of harvesting a fresh stockpile of dark deeds to stack up against their soul. Unfortunately, due to the inability of the law to even begin to deal with such an unprecedented event and its consequences, usually no murder charges could be enforced, so most murders were deemed as suicide.

In certain countries, the law began to prosecute living individuals for taking their own life. Other's claimed on their life insurance. Families cashed-in, wiped out debt and skipped the country. Everything began to fall apart and crime soared as unregistered twins provided irrefutable and iron-clad alibi's to their own crimes. As for myself, I just reached for the bottle that dreaded day of bilocation and crawled inside.

Theories for the event varied, but science ultimately failed to explain and within eighteen months life was back to normal. That is to say, the unresolved problem was roundly ignored by the day to day grind of the banal. Something like a miracle had swift become an obstacle to everyday existence. It paled, as miracles often do, into jaded disbelief and that other unquestionable fact of the human condition; that *shit happens.*

Chapter 2

The sunlight glared off the sidewalk, blinding me. I had to squint and mosey back to the office, mulling over the sterile qualities of my grey existence, passing by the tall, guarded gates of the major studios; those industrial factories of the manufactured dream. Many tourists come to Hollywood to discover a worn out fuck-pit. I mean, it is *immensely* disappointing to the outsider. There's no glamour here, only a cancerous industry. Most people fail to realize that Hollywood is just a machine that churns and turns and shits out films and stupid celebrities. Why in the hell anybody would want to get inside this huge stinking anus was beyond me, but it held a slick, sick fascination for the outsider and the odious cinematic *wannabes*.

Weaving about the sidewalk, I soon realized that I was more tanked than I thought. I was mumbling to myself, spitting and cursing. Each time I tried to focus, my legs would turn rubber and my feet become lead. The sun beat my eyes, the world skipped and span and the slow rise of nausea overcame me. I accidentally puked, but played it cool, trying to mask the beery, noodle-infested spew gurgling from my mouth and down my shirt. I wiped it away with a casual nonchalance, even as I spewed liquid over my hand. *Christ, keep it together!* And then, some luck! I spied a nearby alleyway and ducked down to heave.

It was there, doubled over and speaking Dutch, that I noticed him.

He was a short and scrawny man, wearing a faded purple T-shirt and scruffy jeans. His left arm was bandaged with brown-stained tatters of surgical dressing and he scratched at the raw skin revealed through the gauze, betraying an angry track of needle holes. Occasionally a word exploded out of his mouth. It was random and seemingly pointless to any world but his. The little rat kept looking at me, shifting about on the spot as if he needed to take a leak. A nervy, agitated little bastard, for sure – *but what did he want?*

My head began to feel better. The world settled, but the light still hurt my eyes. I decided to head over to Ding Dong's, a favorite bar haunt of mine and a port in the storm, to gather my thoughts and maybe take a drink or two.

The scrawny man followed.

Chapter 3

Spitting noodles, I trudged along. I felt like Sisyphus and my life the rock. Every goddamn day it was there, right in front of me, demanding that I push hard on a road to nowhere. And at twilight, the rock of my being was right back at the bottom of that steep climb to unrealized dreams and a fresh round of cliché ridden narration. Why in the hell couldn't I turn this wearisome inner monologue off? It even happened as I slept. I'd be fast asleep and then hear something like, '*I slept like a log that night*', which would then wake me up! I thought about seeking professional help about the matter. I even called a therapist, but then hearing the words '*I was nuttier than a wagon-load of pralines*' put me off and I hung up. That on-the-spot diagnosis from my own psychotic condition was a sure sign this mental collapse shouldn't be fucked with and left the hell alone – but I digress.

I heard the scrawny man shout 'TITS!' as he followed close behind. Who was this fool? Why was he on my tail? Obviously an addict in need of some crack money, but all I had was a wrinkled and grimy looking twenty dollar bill. In fact, it was all the money I had in the world and I intended to drink it away at Ding Dong's. I picked up speed. He sloped after me, scratching his arm and cursing Jesus.

Now, Ding Dong Annie's was a bar where all the wannabe screenwriter's mooched about doing anything but writing. They just talked a lot, like most wannabes. Comparing ideas, talking about the script they were developing, ripping apart produced work as their own dismal efforts languished despite their latest script being with *this* celebrity or *that* studio. In other words they talked shit and lied, because the fantasy was as close to the reality they would ever get. I hated them. As I approached the bar I heard one guy say, 'My script is basically like *The Exorcist* meets *The Godfather!*'

I zoned out. They all spoke in pitches, and bad pitches at that. *Christ!*

Ding Dong Annie met me at the bar. Her real name was Sue, but Ding Dong suited her. I don't know where the "Annie" part came from. Anyway, she was stacked and fruity. A voluptuous feast of ebony curves. She was also a former client of mine. I had spied on her husband cheating on Ding with a busty redhead in the back seat of his car. Of course, the lousy deal was that I was busy screwing Ding Dong at the time, but she wanted to nail his ass in a quick divorce. I needed the money, and Ding Dong's a great fuck.

'Tommy Storm,' said Ding, 'how's the "dick" business?'

'Fine,' I said, leaning casually on the bar. 'Thanks for asking. You never returned my calls.'

She shrugged. 'I've been busy, Tommy. What can I say?'

'You can say whatever you want, baby, I'm all ears. And other things,' I twinkled, gamely.

Ding Dong smiled. She liked to feel that I wanted her, no matter what. She liked to feel this sense of power over a man. That with a single, well-placed look she could get my dick dancing like Fred Astaire.

'Mm, Tommy Storm,' she cooed, leaning across the bar, her ebony cleavage rising, 'what can I do for you, honey?'

'Ding Dong,' I said, 'I got some guy tailing me. In fact it's this guy, right here!' I turned to introduce her to the crack head at my side.

'I just fucked a movie star,' said the scrawny man, now standing at my side.

Ding and I cast an uneasy glance over this weirdly animated cadaver. He was grinning, his bulbous eyes trembling in their sockets, his cracked lips masked by a wiry scrub of moustache, faintly tracing down to his chin with an almost pre-pubescent irregularity. His teeth were yellow, his breath stank, his body reeked of defecation and blood and his fingernails never stopped scratching at the stomach turning, now skinless and needle-pocked *malaise* beneath the dressing on his arm.

'I *fucked* a movie star!' he repeated.

'Who was it?' asked Ding Dong, for which I could have slapped her.

'Jesus, this asshole has been on my tail for the last hour! He's following me!'

'I got to follow someone to know where I'm going,' said the scrawny man.

Ding laughed. I rolled my eyes.

'I don't think you need worry, Tommy,' said Ding. 'You want a drink, mister?'

The scrawny man nodded. 'Yes, ma'am, but I don't have any money.'

'Buy him a drink, Tommy?'

'What the hell for? He's not *with* me, he *followed* me! *You* buy him a drink!'

'So shines a good deed in a naughty world,' said the scrawny man.

'Shakespeare,' observed Ding. She looked me square in the eye. 'Our friend can recite *Shakespeare*, Tommy. Can *you* recite Shakespeare?'

'No,' I growled, swigging from my bottle.

She needled me some more, leaning across the bar, fixing me with a mischievous look. 'Buy him a drink, for me?' She fixed me with the look. My dick twitched.

'Fine, here, take my money and buy this stupid asshole a drink!' I pushed the change across the bar towards her. She smiled, reached out and placed a hand on mine, gently squeezing before turning to fix another beer.

'How can you manage to quote Shakespeare, but not know where the hell you're going?' I asked him.

'I just remember it,' he said, nervously shifting about. 'The Merchant of Venice, Act Five. Portia says it – just before she's fucked up the ass.'

Ding placed the beer before the scrawny man. 'I don't remember Portia getting a back door visit in The Merchant of Venice.' She then placed a second beer before me, 'On the house, for being a good guy.'

'You know Shakespeare?' I asked Ding.

'Sure, well, bits of his work. You know, from films.'

'Films,' I groaned, returning to my beer.

'What's wrong with the movies?' she asked.

'You want a list?'

'Well, seeing as you can't quote Shakespeare.'

'We don't have all day. Ask me what I *like* about movies instead.'

'Okay, what do you *like* about movies?'

'Nothing,' I drawled into the bottle neck, taking another swig.

'I fucked a movie star,' sighed the scrawny man, 'and her huge fucking tits were ripe.' He giggled to himself, wiping away a slug of mucus crawling from his nose.

'Who are you?' I asked. 'What's your name? I mean on your home planet?'

'Dave,' he replied. 'My name's Dave.'

'And why are you following me, Dave. And don't give me any of that "I got to follow somebody to know where I'm going!" bullshit.'

Dave shrugged and muttered. 'I can't say, for sure.'

'So...' I began, but then realized the double meaning of his response. 'No, wait, does that mean you don't know or you just can't tell me?'

'I don't know' Dave shrugged and drank his beer.

'Right, so...' He'd done it again. 'Wait, you don't know why you're following me or you don't know what I mean?'

'Jesus, Tommy, let the guy enjoy his beer!'

'That I paid for!' Christ, this was like being back at Woo's all over again! 'Dave, do you actually know why you are following me?'

'Well, I *fucked* a movie star,' he re-announced with a smile. 'And fucking her was like coring the stone out of a split peach, sir! She took it every fucking way this side of Christmas! Dirty bitch even bruised my balls. You want to see?' He went for his trousers.

'No,' I said.

He then played it cool. 'Maybe I'll see her again, I don't know.'

'Fascinating,' Ding sighed. 'Let me get you guys another drink.'

'Hey wait a second!' I called after her. 'This asshole isn't with me! He's not my friend!'

'You sound shocked,' torpedoed the response from the back room.

'Tits,' said Dave, scratching his arm.

Ding returned with a bottle of bourbon and three glasses, placing them on the bar and then pouring. 'On the house,' she said, shooting a 'Happy?' in my direction.

'Ecstatic,' I growled.

Dave reached for the glass and proposed a toast to big tits.

Ding opted, 'What about new acquaintances?'

'And big tits,' said Dave.

'No,' she said flatly 'to new acquaintances, or get out.'

Dave became meek. He toasted. I thought what the hell and toasted Dave as well, swallowing the bourbon in one.

'There,' said Ding Dong. 'Now, Dave, head on home like a good boy. I have some unfinished business with Mr Storm.'

She looked at me again and my dick duly danced.

Had I known any better, I would have killed that son of a bitch Dave there and then.

Chapter 4

Up in the bedroom, I cupped one of Ding Dong's breasts in my right hand. She was busy working me, riding me like a cheap fairground ride. I wondered what the hell she saw in a man like me. I wasn't exactly Grade-A material for a woman of her caliber.

'God you're dick is big!' she yelled.

Well, I guess that figured it, I thought.

After the fun and games we lay in bed together. A fine example of racial harmony, I thought.

'You know, your friend down there...'

'He's *not* my friend,' I cut in.

'Whatever. He looks familiar.'

'Maybe you served him before?'

'I doubt it. God, he looks familiar. Shit, this is going to drive me nuts!'

'Don't worry about it. You'll remember. It'll just come to you when you least expect it. Like the clap.'

'Like the what?'

'Oh, nothing' I mumbled.

A thought suddenly flipped into her head. She grimaced. 'God, that bandage! I thought I was going to puke!'

I sighed and nodded. 'Poor bastard,' I said, 'this fucking town gets everyone in the end.'

'Yeah,' said Ding Dong, softly. I felt her pull me a little closer. 'That's what I like about you, Tommy.'

'What?'

'Underneath the bullshit, you got a heart.'

I looked into her eyes. I held her gaze for a good while then said, 'I'll pretend I didn't hear that.'

She laughed. We kissed. We hugged. The hug became an embrace and we screwed again.

After an hour or so we made my way back downstairs into the

bar. We both noticed Dave lurking outside on the other side of the street, pacing up and down the sidewalk, halting opposite the bar every time the door opened, craning his neck and peering in to get a clear view of me. Well, I wasn't going anywhere. Whatever this daffy bastard was up to could wait. I was enjoying some quality time with Ding, but she was still distracted.

'Damn, he reminds me of someone' she said to me, serving drinks to an old poet, down on his luck.

'Dave?'

'Yeah,' she added, her voice tinged with an air of the absent-minded.

'Maybe, maybe,' I added. 'He's not the sort you forget easy.'

She finished serving the poet, who retreated into a lonely corner to shell peanuts and write on scraps of paper.

'It's annoying me. I know him from someplace, I'm sure of it!'

'It'll come to you. Forget it,' I opined, with the unmistakable confidence of a man with no fucking idea worth a damn.

'Another?' she asked, retrieving my empty bottle.

I sighed. 'I'm flat broke. That's it until the next payment rolls in.'

'Which is when?'

I shrugged and looked pathetic, hoping to score a free drink, perhaps even a little sympathy, a sign of affection or glance of feeling from those big, hazel-colored eyes. Hoping to see my luck turn on its worn out heels.

'I guess you're not paying your tab tonight, then?'

All I saw in her eyes was a sudden, familiar weariness that broke my heart, and I knew that behind the smiles and cheerful façade, she already had my number.

'I promise, as soon as I get my money. I'm still chasing back payments!' I lied. 'Soon, I promise. I always pay my debts.'

She nodded, her trust given. 'Okay, Tommy.'

I smiled, but inside I was recoiling in horror at the knife I just planted in her back. I was no good. No good at all. My soul was cunning by nature. It wasn't my fault.

After a while I checked the time, it was getting late, so I made my excuses and left. Guilt pushed me out of the bar and into the streets where I belonged. I decided to head back to the office.

Dave followed.

Chapter 5

After that gross betrayal against the woman I loved, I needed another drink. I made my way over to a small bar where they hadn't sussed me as a serial liability and the owner, a former client, owed a few favors. I managed to squeeze a few drinks from him, but my mouth was running over and my attitude became ballsy. I began demanding drinks from the bar staff.

'Beer,' I ordered, slapping my palm hard on the bar.

'Yes, sir!' said the young barkeep, saluting sharply before giving me the finger. 'Would you also like to fuck my mother?'

'I *have* fucked your mother,' said I, 'and she gives lousy head. Now give me a fucking beer before we take this thing outside.'

'Then let's take it outside, you old fart,' said the barkeep, and he leapt over the bar.

I laughed, summoning up what was left of my wafer-thin courage. 'You know I could kick your ass all over this town, kid?'

'Fine by me,' he said, unfazed. 'And it's a city, you senile fuck!'

'I'm serious,' I reiterated, 'you fuck with me and you end up in the gutter. You really want to go that route, kid?'

He shrugged, 'Yeah, why not? I've finished my shift. My evening's free. Let's go, old man.'

'Fine,' said I, removing my jacket. 'Let's step outside.'

We fought long and hard down the back of the bar. We threw punches, we kicked, we wrestled and each man took a fair share of abuse. Blood began to flow, but mostly from me. In the end I stepped back, exhausted of getting my ass kicked.

'This isn't worth a beer,' I said.

'It's not about the beer,' said the barkeep. 'It's about your attitude. You're a fucking jerk.'

'Christ, kid, I was feeling cocky and full of myself. You know how it is after a few drinks. Look, I apologize, okay?'

He thought about this for a moment, and then said, 'Okay, let me buy you that beer.'

'Thanks anyway, kid, but I'm heading home.'

'Fine,' said the barkeep.

We made our peace. Sometimes when you fight a man, you develop a mutual respect. Sometimes you need to earn your friends in this life.

'One thing,' the kid said, getting close and jabbing his finger into my chest to make a point, 'If you *ever* talk to me like that again, I *will* smash your face in, split your fucking skull and use it as an ashtray. You understand me, shithead?'

'Sure thing, kid,' I said, patting him on the arm, a friendly smile for good measure.

The kid held my gaze for a moment before punching me in the gut. I doubled over, gasping for breath and hit the floor.

'Patronizing bastard,' he spat, leaving me in the dirt.

Damn thing is, I was actually being sincere. I really liked the kid.

Chapter 6

'Hi,' said Dave, looking down at me. 'You want some help?'

'No, really, I'm fine. Thank you.'

Dave nodded then looked about nervously, all shifting feet and arm scratching.

'It's fine, really,' I repeated.

'Yeah,' said Dave, smiling goofy. 'Hey, I fucked a movie star tonight. You know that?'

'You told me,' I answered flatly, resting my head on the cold concrete floor and gazing up at where the stars used to be.

'She had big tits,' said Dave.

I sighed. 'How big, Dave?'

'They were just incredible, sir. That's all I can say on the matter.'

'I see. So why aren't you there now, humping her ass?'

'She's got work in the morning,' said Dave, in a matter of fact tone. 'She said she'd call me. It's cool.'

'I envy you, Dave. I truly do.'

'Yeah,' he said quietly. Then, as an afterthought, he followed up with a distant, 'Pecker juice.'

'Jesus Christ!' I groaned, easing myself up off the floor and brushing myself down. I retrieved my faithful Berkeley and dropped it onto my head.

'Where are you headed?' asked Dave.

'I'm going home, Dave. See you around.' And I limped away. Dave followed.

About a block from the office I turned around.

'Look, you crazy fucker, what exactly do you want?'

Dave just looked at me.

'Okay, fine,' I said. 'Let's find an ATM. I'll prove my poverty!'

Dave followed me across the street to the nearest cashpoint. I jammed my card angrily into the slot and stabbed the numbers into the keypad.

'I don't even have enough money for food, never mind the rent!' I whined.

'Her gash,' said Dave, shaking his head and laughing. 'Man, what a gash!'

I was no longer listening. Instead I was staring at the screen in disbelief. My account was now fifty thousand dollars in the black.

'And her tits were *huge*! You know that? Did I tell you I fucked a movie star tonight? That's what I'm talking about,' said Dave, 'big tits!'

'*Fuck* her tits, Dave!'

'I did,' he chuckled on. 'Oh man, like screwing ass, only you could see your pecker between the—'

'Goddamn it, shut up, would you? I need to think here.'

What in the hell had happened? And why had I nobody else but Dave to share this momentous event with? By my lousy standards, I was a rich man.

'Here,' I said, handing Dave a generous bribe. 'Fuck off.'

Dave stood there for a time, examining the bill. Then he just walked off, scratching at his arm and leaving his stink in his wake.

I watched him vanish. I breathed a sigh of relief. I then decided to get my ass back to the office and think things through.

Chapter 7

Back at the office I discovered I wasn't there. I tried calling myself but I wasn't answering my own cell phone. Where in the hell was I? Did I even know about the money in my account?

The pain growled in my bruised ribs and battered face. I sat down in the worn and scuffed red leather chair, kicking my feet up onto the paper-strewn desk, groaning a little with the effort and then opening a drawer to pull out a half bottle of scotch. I unscrewed the cap and took a hit, my split lip stinging at the neat wash of alcohol. My conscience burned like a fire in my skull, a hot coal rattling about the empty bone chamber, jostling for space against the rat-shaped genius of my own arrogance and self-preservation.

Christ, I was a piece of work! Ignoble in reason, finite in faculties – save for covering my ass – and now dabbing blood from my mouth with a used tissue, having already spotted my puke-stained shirt with tiny red medals of drinker's courage. I was lower than the angels, for sure, and as far from God as the rotten universe could shit me out. This life, so it seemed, was pointless and absurd. Where was hope? Where was the Almighty?

The phone rang. I answered. A plummy, English voice replied to my surly greeting, saying, 'Hello, Mr Storm, it's Anthony Prendergast here.'

'What?' I shot back, taking another hit from the bottle. 'Who is this? Speak up!'

'*Anthony Prendergast*,' confirmed the voice. 'I hired you to find the whereabouts of my daughter, remember? I'm calling to see if you've made any progress?'

'Do you know what time it is?'

'It's late I know. I'm sorry to call.'

'No,' I slurred, 'I think my watch has broken. Do you know

what time it is?'

'Oh,' said Prendergast, 'It's eleven-thirty.'

Christ, I'd been drinking for hours. I figured I'd carry on and eventually drink myself sober. I took another hit of scotch. The room began to spin. I felt exhausted.

'So, is there any news on my daughter?'

'I'm on the case,' I said, my breathing labored. 'Leave it with me. I'm following up a number of leads. In fact, I just got back from following some guy who might know something,' I lied, before quickly covering myself for any follow up questions with, 'but I can't mention any names, in case my phone is tapped. The criminal underwear is smart.'

'Criminal underwear, did you say?'

'No, I said *criminal underworld*. Is there a problem with your hearing? If so, tell me. Don't be shy. We can work around it.'

'My hearing is fine, Mr Storm.'

'Good, good,' I said, holding the bottle in the air before me, swilling the scotch around and enjoying the swish of liquor in the glass. 'Call me tomorrow morning. I'll have some more information for you then. Goodnight.'

'Just a moment, please,' said Prendergast. 'I'd like you to come over to my house tomorrow, if that's convenient? There's something I need to discuss with you in person.'

'Can't you come here?'

'I'm sorry, Mr Storm, but I'm a very busy man and this is of paramount importance.'

'You work for Paramount?' I enquired.

'It's a figure of speech,' he explained, 'akin to a turn of phrase?'

'A turn of phrase,' I repeated. I liked that. I'd have to work that into conversation, sometime.

'I'll send a car for you. Let's say, eleven-thirty? Twelve hours from now? Ah, I like the symmetry of that! Yes, most agreeable.'

'Yeah, I guess.'

'Excellent! My driver will meet you outside the office at the allotted time. Please wear a tie. Thank you and goodnight.'

The line went dead. The office suddenly felt unnaturally quiet and still.

Ten minutes later the phone rang again. I answered, as drunk as hell, my words falling onto the desk like lead weights. An all-too-familiar voice croaked back, like a toad from hell.

'Storm, this is Jake. I'm calling about the rent.'

'You'll have it by the end of the week,' I said, mangling my words as I lifted the bottle to my cracked lips.

'You said that five weeks ago, Storm. I've given you enough time here. You've left me with no option. I'm going to have to send the Boys round.'

'Fine, so send them, Jake. Send them now if you dare.'

'Oh I will, Storm. You can be goddamn certain of that, you cocky little shit-stain. I'm going to call them right now. Your ass is for the gutter, buddy.'

He hung up. I leaned back in the chair, opened up the desk drawer and took a hit from a bottle of bourbon resting in there for times like this; times when a man, faced with insurmountable odds, has to take it on the chin and face the music. Wait, now I had two bottles, which momentarily confused me, but somehow kicked my booze-sodden brain into remembering that I had fifty thousand bucks in my account. I'd just razzed Jake for nothing and now the touchy son-of-a-bitch was sending the Boys over to work my ass like dough for the oven.

I grabbed the phone and dialed Jake's number. I was so drunk my hands felt huge, stricken with gigantism. My fingers now transformed into colossal wieners.

'Hello?'

'Jake, it's Storm.'

'You've got some nerve, Storm! Well, tough shit, pal, the Boys are on their way!'

'Listen, Jake, there's been a mistake here.'

'Oh really, wise ass?'

'Yeah, listen, I was only joking, see? I have the money. I have it all plus next month's rent in advance. I'll deliver it personally.' I was suddenly very sober.

'Oh *please*, Storm,' Jake laughed, 'you don't have it and then in the space of three minutes you have it again?'

'That's pretty much it, yeah.'

'You're full of shit.'

I heard the line go dead. I redialed.

'Hello?'

'Don't hang up, *please*,' I implored. 'I *have* the money, Jake. I swear to Christ I have it!'

There was a long silence, then, 'You *seriously* have it?'

'Yes!'

Another long silence, and then, 'Okay, Storm. I'll be around tomorrow for the rent. I'll call the Boys, let them know.'

'Thanks, Jake. I appreciate it.'

'I don't have a sense of humor when it comes to my money, Storm. Remember that in future. Keep your stupid jokes for your fucking Judaic whatever.'

'Duly noted, Jake, and thanks,' I said, breathing a sigh of relief.

Three minutes later the phone rang.

'Storm, I can't reach them.'

'Reach them?' I echoed.

'The Boys,' he explained.

'Shit.'

'Don't worry. I'll keep trying. They probably have their cell phones turned off. They think it adds to global warming or some shit like that. I'll keep trying them.'

Jake hung up. I sat at the desk unable to move, the weight upon my shoulders.

And lo, the phone rang once more.

'Hello?' I answered, cautiously.

'Thomas Storm?' said a deep voice. 'I'm one of the Boys. We're on our way, motherfucker. We're *real* close.'

'Now wait a second! I just talked to Jake...'

He cut in. 'I'm sure you did, bitch. *Game over.*'

The line went dead.

I immediately called Jake back.

'They're on their way.'

'They are?' said Jake. 'Did you ask them to call me?'

'What? No! They wouldn't listen to me, for Christ's sake! Do something!'

'Okay, okay, take it easy. I'll try them again. Obviously their phone is on now, right?'

'Right,' I said.

'So take it easy, okay? Christ, you wouldn't be in this predicament if you hadn't been such a smart ass, Storm. See what I mean, now?'

Jake hung up. I sat at the desk and waited.

The phone rang. I answered.

'Bitch,' said the deep male voice, bristling with threat.

'Is that you, mom?' I replied.

'My associate and I have been discussing what to do with your sorry white ass.'

'Okay,' I said.

'You know what I've got in my hands?'

'A puppy?'

'*Pliers*, fuck-wit!' shot the reply. 'You ever had your balls fucked up with pliers, bitch?'

I said nothing. What could I say?

'These pliers have seen a lot of pink flesh, Storm. They've cut dicks, assholes and eyelids a-plenty, but for you I'm thinking of your balls. I will *peel* your balls with these pliers, fucker. And when I'm finished, when you're on the floor, holding your sack, your hands covered in blood and you can do nothing but fucking scream, then I'll piss in your mouth. And when I piss in your screaming mouth, fucker, it's going to feel like the best goddamn thing in the world. 'Cause when I go to work on your balls with these here pliers, I'm going to make sure that I shove these rusty fuckers up the end of your dick shaft and open them up real wide, real slow.'

'So, you know my ex, then?' I said, putting on a brave face.

'We're real close now.'

'Okay. Do I get a last request?'

'No, baby, because you'll live on. You'll wish you were dead, sure, but there's no requests, no favors. We're turning the corner right now, baby. I can see your office. Here we come.'

I almost wet myself as the fear shook my spine. I staggered over to the window and, sure enough, there was a large black car pulling up outside.

'Ring Jake,' I said, trying not to retch. 'He wants to call it off.'

'You're funny. I'm laughing. Can you hear me laughing?'

I heard nothing.

'See you soon.'

I dropped the phone. I had no choice. I had to run. Jake had let me down. I grabbed my keys, the bottle of scotch, my Berkeley and made tracks.

Chapter 8

I was three floors down when I met up with them.

'The Boys' were two very large African-American gentlemen. They wore black leather jackets into which muscle was packed tight. One had a nose ring and the other an effeminate looking moustache and plucked eyebrows. I never got to know them personally, you understand, so let's just refer to them as Nose Ring and Pliers.

'Storm,' said Nose Ring, as Pliers lived up to his name, brandishing the evil-looking fuckers in the air between us.

'Boys,' said I, brandishing the scotch. 'Care for a drink?'

'Shut the fuck up!' screamed Pliers.

'Well, then,' I began, swigging from the bottle, 'how shall we do this thing?'

Now, to my credit, I tried to get past them. I planted the bottle of scotch over Nose Ring's head but Pliers punched me in the gut and I went down. He followed up by kicking me in the face. They hauled me back up the steps and back into the office where they beat the shit out of me.

And then Nose Ring pinned me to the office desk. I gagged and struggled as his hand squeezed my throat. Luckily, Pliers didn't interfere with my balls straight off, I'm glad to say. Instead he just cut up the fingers on my left hand. Crying and screaming in agony, I forgot to thank God for saving my nuts.

'Enough,' said Nose Ring, releasing his grip and stepping back.

Pliers backed off. My hand was dripping blood and ablaze with pain. He'd done a good job.

The boy's cell phone suddenly rang. It played a jaunty little number. Nose Ring looked at the caller display, sighed 'Fuck!' and then answered. On the other end was Jake.

Pliers dutifully patched me up as Nose Ring spoke with Jake

on the phone. Jake was decent enough to take the rent owed and not a month in advance as I suggested. He'd call round tomorrow afternoon at three. Cash only, of course. *What a sport,* I thought. *What a hell of a decent guy.*

Meanwhile, the skin had been snipped on all the fingers of my left hand and to cap it all Pliers cheerfully informed me the digit job was merely the appetizer to the main course: the destruction of my balls. He added that I was very, very fortunate.

'Yeah, blessed,' I said, wiping away the tears and dignity.

'Hell, don't worry,' said Pliers. 'They all cry the first time!'

'And the second time, what then?'

He smiled. 'There is no "second time", baby.' And the bastard laughed right in my face.

Chapter 9

Blissfully ignorant of my fate, I drank on through pain and beyond the night into the brazen arrival of another L.A. dawn.

The things that cross your mind in the early hours, when alcohol brings out the qualities of the mystic and philosopher, talking to yourself as you pace the room, grappling with inner demons and anxieties, smelt in the disgusting furnace of burning shame. It's enough to make a man take a dive out of his window. I actually considered it, but was in two minds as to whether or not I could, in my wretched condition, actually succeed in killing myself or spend the rest of my days feeding through a straw as some buxom nurse with golden thighs teased my lifeless prick for kicks. These things happened, apparently.

Skipping breakfast, I walked the streets in a daze, my hand throbbing with pain, my head heavy and stale with drink. My life was a mess, but then I was a child of Los Angeles, so I figured it was as natural as smog, fake tits and Botox.

'I fucked a movie star!'

My heart sank. I turned around and there he was, scuttling along behind me like a traumatized crab, chattering to the breeze, scratching at his scabs, his crazy eyes roaming, popping out of his ghastly skull wrapped in a thin layer of tight flesh. Blue veins branched from his temples like thin horns, tattoo close and networking through that sallow sack of skull and madness. What a cunt.

'I fucked her with my stinger!' laughed Dave, squealing with delight at the image. Then he called after me, hobbling over to my side. 'Hey, wait! Wait! I fucked a movie star, listen! I fucked her with my *stinger*! Like a stinging wasp!'

'Please,' I began, feeling my body sag under the weight of Dave's company, 'just leave me alone!'

Dave looked perplexed. 'I can't. How can I?'

'Can't what? Can't leave me alone or can't figure out how to do it? Jesus, you speak in riddles!'

Dave got touchy. 'Maybe you just hear in them!' And with that, he was gone, running up the street.

I trudged back to the office for my rendezvous with Prendergast's driver.

Chapter 10

The back of the limousine had a strong smell of newly waxed leather. The odor was not unpleasant, but slightly overpowering, so I opened the window a crack, allowing the breeze to dance across my face, refreshing my tired eyes and dispelling the rich stink of wealth.

'I understand you are a private investigator, sir?' queried the old boy driving me to *chez Prendergast*.

'I am indeed. Name's Tommy Storm, you ever heard of me?'

'No, sir,' he replied.

'I'm quite well-known,' I lied. 'A little unconventional, sure, but I get the job done.' Pure bullshit!

'Mr Prendergast will be most glad to hear that,' said the old boy, watching me in the rearview mirror, his withered eyes casting a suspect glance over my person.

'Eyes on the road, Jeeves,' I said. 'We wouldn't want an accident now, would we?'

His eyes shifted back onto the road and I allowed myself a moment of hubris, opening the window some more so that the people might better see my face.

Look at me, you turds!

After a while, the car turned into a long driveway with an automated gate that closed silently behind us. The car slowed to a gentle stop outside the marble steps of the Prendergast mansion. It resembled a cheesy Hollywood movie set of ancient Rome. A statue of Zeus, nobly reaching to the heavens, face set in stern countenance, was set by the large double doors that slowly opened as I climbed the steps. Out stepped a small, neatly dressed man with round glasses and a scrub of wiry grey hair.

'Tommy Storm,' said Prendergast, putting forth an open hand, 'it's so good to see you again.'

I shook the podgy, stunted paw. His grip was non-existent, but the touch of his skin gave me the creeps, as though I were shaking hands with a known child-abusing mass murderer. I figured all producers elicited the same response in people; like lawyers, dentists and my uncle Levi, who was a therapist in Beverley Hills until the law got wind of his lack of credentials. Not to mention his unprofessional stance that "therapist" was actually a condensed form of "the rapist" and thus an acceptable form of therapy. And he still charged by the half hour, but that's another story.

'Please, this way,' said Prendergast, ushering me away from the door and around the side of the house into his garden.

The garden was a vibrant shock of crisp psychedelic colors, zephyr-kissed and bright shining under the L.A. sun. Amid this alarming blaze of color, a furious buzz of insects, thrashed the air with their wings and zipped past my ears like lead wasps. It was an unnerving place to be. As if there was simply *too much* life there. I began to sweat with panic, my throat clawing for a drink to calm my pounding heart.

'So,' began Prendergast, 'I presume you have the first installment of the agreed payment.'

I dimly remembered the money in my account. 'Yeah, it's there. Thanks.'

'Excellent,' he continued, offering me a pristine cotton handkerchief. 'Here, use this.'

I took the handkerchief and mopped my face. Insects, once sticking to my perspiration, now mangled in the sweaty cotton death of my hosts generosity. Christ, what a world.

'Mr Storm, being touched by the quantum irregularity now gripping our world, I find you entirely fascinating. '

'What?'

'The quantum irregularity of W-Day, the grand bilocation of individuals in the same way a light photon can be both a wave and a particle *at the same time*. Fascinating! A friend of mine is also graced with the condition. God knows I'm no scientist, but it seems to be an unfolding of the universe as we know it! Things are not set in stone and mystery, true mystery, prevails! Ah, what times we live in!'

I sighed, swatting bugs on my neck, desperate to get down to business so I could escape this fucking insect house.

He droned on. 'Could it be the next step in the evolution of the universe? God, it is very freeing, isn't it?'

'Freeing?' This statement puzzled me.

'It feels like the laws are being, dare I say it, smashed? Broken? The rules of the game are changing, Mr Storm.'

'What game?'

'The game of life,' he said.

'You think life is a game?'

'Don't you?'

'I think life deals a lousy hand, but I wouldn't call it a game.'

'That's interesting.'

This conversation was beginning to spook me. I decided to change the subject.

'So,' I grasped, 'you made that film about the homosexual Jewish toreador.'

'Yes!' he piped excitedly. 'Did you like it?'

'Well, I never actually—'

'You know,' he cut in with a chuckle, 'there's a *very* amusing story about how that film came about.'

I suddenly yearned for death.

Chapter 11

After boring me with his story, Prendergast continued to accompany me around his garden. It was a haven to strange, exotic looking flowers. The insects swarmed over stamen and petal, hungry for nectar and pollen.

'All unique hybrids,' he explained. 'They cost me a small fortune.'

The smell was overpowering. I felt sick. And with the audible buzz of the insects, I felt a little dizzy. It was a horrible place to be.

'My daughter,' he finally said, 'is very young and naturally inexperienced. Her infatuation is merely that of a child. It is not to be taken into consideration during the course of your investigation.'

'Just tell me who she's fucking,' I blurted, quickly correcting myself, 'I mean, who she is seeing. I have contacts. People that work in the industry. I can make some calls, maybe glean some information.'

'Absolutely *not*,' said Prendergast firmly. 'This is a matter of discretion, Mr Storm. You start asking questions to the wrong people and the papers will soon get wind of it. We have a very large film coming out in the summer. We are banking on this film to *make money*. A lot of personal favors were called in to get this project off the ground.' Prendergast seemed a little uptight about the matter. 'My *reputation* is on the line.'

I nodded to myself. I had found his weakness.

Prendergast swatted the worries aside, saying, 'Politics of the studio system. Not a problem for you to worry about. And count your lucky stars for it.'

My attention focused on the constant, dull throb of pain in my left hand. That was the second time today I'd been lucky, thought lucky old me.

I decided to compromise. 'Okay, what about your daughter?'

'What about my daughter? I've already given you – that is to say, the other you – all the necessary details.' Prendergast smelled a rat. 'There's nothing *wrong* is there, Mr Storm?'

'Not at all,' I covered. 'Only I've been working another case and not been able to catch up with myself, so to speak. A copy of the information you gave to me would be a big help, you know?'

Prendergast smiled. 'That's not a problem. I'll email it over. Now, allow me to show you something truly unique.'

At the far end of the garden was a miniature orchard. Prendergast strode ahead to stand by his pride and joy.

'Nice apples,' I quipped.

'Never mind the apples,' said Prendergast, 'what do you make of *that*?' thumbing at the object behind him, set amongst the orchard.

It looked like a statue. I said so. He nodded, so I was right I guess. However, there was more.

'This statue is one of the few examples of early Gnostic-Christian art. It represents one of...'

I zoned out again. I couldn't give a flying fuck, but I played along, nodding like a fucking moron as Prendergast continued.

'According to Gnostic belief, this world was created by the demiurge; a deity born by chance within creation and ignorant of the reality of *the* real God, if you will.'

'Okay,' I said.

'The God that made this world – in fact the material universe – is a fraud in Gnostic tradition.'

'Okay,' I said again.

Prendergast laughed. 'Well, that's what the screenplay says! No, Mr Storm, this is actually a prop from my latest sci-fi film! I thought it made rather a nice feature for my garden, don't you think?'

I glanced over the statue, pretending to admire the crafts-manship but really just taking a moment to swallow the fact that

Prendergast was a complete asshole. He was tedious, boring and utterly incapable of *not* drawing attention to himself and his work for more than five minutes.

'Sounds an interesting film,' I lied. 'What's it called?'

'*The Dark Mind,*' said Prendergast. 'It is *the* big film of the summer. That's why I need you to resolve this matter as quickly as possible. If the press gets wind of this the damage to my film will be irreparable. My leading actor is a respected family man. Well, that's how he's *marketed* anyway.'

His smile faded. He reminded me of that old serpent in Paradise. Those beady eyes fixed onto me. Prendergast was serious.

'Time frame,' I demanded.

'You have a week. Seven days from now. You've already been paid half up front. The rest will follow on completion of the assignment.'

'I'm on the case,' I said, tipping my Berkeley and walking back through the garden. My big exit ruined by the countless bugs stuck to my face.

Chapter 12

Wiping the bugs off, I soon discovered that Prendergast's driver had given me a lift out into the Hills, but was reluctant to take me back.

'I was asked to pick you up, smart ass, not take you back.'

'Look, Mr Prendergast said…'

'He said *nothing*,' snapped the old boy. '*Fuck off*.'

So I walked for a time and cursed the old bastard and my smart mouth and then caught the bus back into Hollywood.

On the bus, I reasoned that my sole priority was to find myself and figure out what the hell was going on.

'Hi there,' said a familiar voice behind me.

'Dave?' I said, turning around in my seat. It was he.

'You know that movie star I told you about? The one I fucked?'

'Yeah, I remember,' I said.

Dave leaned close. His stinking breath and rotten arm rose up to greet me. 'We did it again last night.'

'That's great,' I said, humoring him. 'I'm glad you're getting some.'

'Yeah,' Dave sighed, leaning back, grinning. 'Sweetest tits I ever sucked.'

'*Excuse me!*' snapped a woman opposite, putting her arm about her daughter.

'Oh, I'm sorry, ma'am,' said Dave contritely.

'Maybe we should talk about this another time?' I suggested.

'Yeah, yeah,' he whispered, 'sounds good, so what time are you thinking?'

I looked at him. He suddenly had me by the balls. I sure walked into that one. Then again, it was kind of good to see him alive. Even in this state. 'Remember that bar we went into the last night?'

'Uh, yeah, I think.'

'Meet me there at eight tonight. Okay? We'll talk about it then.'

'You promise?' said Dave.

'I promise, yeah.'

'Aw, that's really cool.'

And Dave patted me on the shoulder.

Back at the office I began going through files on the computer, in the filing cabinet, through drawers and old coat pockets trying to source some information on my whereabouts.

Nothing! I remembered that Prendergast was sending me some information. I checked my emails and sure enough, there it was. I downloaded the information and opened the file.

The image of Rochelle Prendergast appeared on screen. She was beautiful. I couldn't take my eyes off her. She had shoulder-length blonde hair and her eyes were clear blue. Her charming smile played about full lips that I could already feel against my own.

'Holy shit!' I said aloud, my dick already swelling in my pants.

Yeah, she was beautiful alright. In fact, she was borderline too beautiful to fuck. Quite how Prendergast had squeezed such quality from those fat testes was beyond my comprehension. I was half-debating jerking off when the phone rang. I answered. It was me.

'Where in the name of sweet *fuck* have you been?' I snapped.

'Shut up and listen, I don't have a lot of time. Has Prendergast been in touch?'

'Yeah, he's been needling me for information. I told him nothing, don't worry.'

'That's because you know nothing,' I shot back. 'You think I'd fuck things up by telling you?'

'Now just a second,' I said, realizing I did have a smart mouth after all, 'you take that back!'

'Listen carefully. Tell Prendergast nothing. I'll be in touch. Go buy a cell phone, text me the number. I'll contact you.'

'What the hell's going on here, Tommy?'

'Remember that film I told you about: the gay Jew toreador movie?'

'Prendergast produced it, yeah.'

'There's an actor in that film called David Cross. He's now a big time star. *That's the guy.*'

Mystery solved. Hey, I was pretty smart when I wanted to be.

'David Cross is not screwing the Prendergast kid.'

'And how can you be so sure?'

'He's gay.'

'And how do you know?'

'He told me.'

'Oh.'

'Yeah, the whole family and marriage thing is a façade, managed by the studio.'

'Where the hell are you?' I asked.

'I can't say right now. I'll call you, I promise. Keep that phone on you at all times and keep it turned on, because this is *big*, Tommy. Trust me.'

'I trust you,' I said. And I did. I never said anything was big unless I meant it. So this was big.

And then I was gone.

I went out and purchased a cheap cell phone. As soon as I could, I sent a text to my other cell phone. I received a text back, saying:

GOT U

All I could do now was to wait.

Chapter 13

'Do you always drink during the day?'

'Only when I'm sober,' I replied, swigging from the bottle of beer.

'That's funny,' said the lanky man with a loud, jovial laugh.

'Fuck you,' I replied.

He laughed some more. I wasn't joking, but whatever. He introduced himself as Tom Rancher. He was a screenwriter.

'Oh, really' I said. 'And what films have you written?'

'I've made a few shorts. I wrote them. My writing partner and I are developing a few feature film projects. We got ourselves an agent and managed to get a script to X-Land Films.'

'So, you've done nothing,' I affirmed.

'I wouldn't say that,' he defended. 'Getting a script to X-Land Films is pretty good.'

I was sick and tired of these fucking deadbeats and their bullshit. Hollywood was full of them. The whole fucking world was full of them. They spread like cancer, like an unstoppable virus, polluting the good clean smoggy air with their stink. I hated them.

'What about you? Are you working on anything at the moment?'

'I just had a screenplay optioned. It's about a man with huge nuts who fucks his mother and the whole world dies of AIDS.'

I waited. I knew he'd *eventually* ask the question.

'Who optioned that?'

'X-Land Films,' I spat, 'now *fuck off.*'

He left me to my bottle.

My head was spinning. I'd come to the Merlin for peace, but crap was hitting me from all sides. The sound of writers that never wrote, vomiting huge pats of shit that attracted all the other flies.

Flies love shit and that's why these wannabes swarmed together. Here, in the anus of the world, puking over their lousy ideas and then sucking it all up again.

'Hi,' said Dave, standing beside me.

I sighed. My bodyweight seemed to quadruple. My frame sagged as tiny men with grappling hooks tried to pull me to the floor, probably expecting me to die. Or, maybe they'd kill me and then fuck each other on my warm corpse, L.A. style.

'Dave,' I said, 'it's not eight o' clock as yet. In fact,' I checked my watch, 'it's only five. You're three hours early.'

'I'm not early' said Dave.

'You're not?'

'No, I'm just killing time here until I meet you at eight.'

I nodded. 'Are you not meeting your film-star lady friend, today?'

He shook his head.

We sat in silence. He scratched his arm. I drank my beer. The damn thing was I actually didn't mind the wacky bastard being there. I was glad of his company. He wasn't annoying me with his tit-fucking talk, he was just there. And sometimes that's all a guy needs to find strength, or a lousy, hard-boiled platitude.

I ordered more beer. I also ordered a bottle for Dave, but he refused it.

'I don't drink,' he said.

I looked at his arm. 'You *don't?*'

He shook his head. I swigged more beer. 'Maybe you should start for a while, give your fucking arm a rest.'

He said nothing.

'Sorry,' I said. 'That was a shitty thing to say. I'm sorry, okay?'

'Why?'

'Never mind,' I said and drank.

I looked up at the clock above the bar. It was six minutes past five.

'My brother,' began Dave, 'he found God.'

'I used to date a girl who found God' I said. 'Every time I fucked her she'd say "Jesus! Jesus! Jesus!"'

Dave just stared at me.

'That was a joke,' I said.

'Yeah,' said Dave, 'he found God. He didn't find Jesus, though. I don't think. I could ask?'

'Probably the best thing to do,' I said. 'Check first.'

Dave nodded dumbly.

I felt like jamming the bottle into his eye socket. I wondered if the beer would come out of his mouth like an ornamental fountain. A new bar feature? I'd run it past Ding Dong.

'Your brother,' I said, half-fearing the question, 'what's he like?'

'He's my twin,' said Dave. 'I love him very much.'

'That's good.'

'You have a brother?'

'Yeah, kind of, I guess. It's complicated.'

'You don't get on?'

I shrugged. 'I've not really seen him of late,' I said, remembering to check my cell phone. There were still no calls. 'Shit,' I muttered and took another drink.

'I don't see my brother much,' said Dave. 'Last time I saw him was two days ago. He's real busy with God these days. I don't believe in God. Do you?'

'No,' I said.

'I mean, he showed me, but I wasn't convinced.' Dave laughed.

'How did he show you?' I was intrigued.

'You know,' said Dave, 'he just *showed* me.'

I lowered my voice. 'What, like it was in his pants or something? Is that what you mean?'

The allusion went over Dave's head. He laughed. 'How can God live in your pants?'

The idea wasn't so stupid to most men.

'Forget it,' I said.

Dave stood up. 'I'll be back here later.' And he walked out, still scratching his arm, the smell of warm blood and raw flesh lingering in the air.

I realized I was drunk. Asking Dave about being sexually molested by his God-bothering brother was a new low, even by my floor-scraping standards. God, what a heel I was. Get a few drinks down me and the sleaze pit bubbled. Sad thing was I had booze down me most of the time. Maybe all these assholes had a point about me being a rude, smart ass?

And why had God, that old greybeard, worked his way into two conversations today? Was this a sign? Was there, in fact, a God watching over me? A guardian angel at my side, hand upon my shoulder, telling me to lay that bottle down and go home and pray. God, I hoped not. That was the lousiest advice I'd ever heard.

'*That's* who he reminds me of!' exclaimed Ding Dong, as I jumped out of my skin.

'Christ, baby! You scared the living shit out of me! Don't do that!'

She sat down next to me, putting her arm about me and kissing me on the cheek. 'Aw, I'm sorry, *private dick*.'

Gee, not heard that one, or a million variants on it, before.

'God, Tommy, how long have you been here?'

'Long enough to get hassled by your asshole clientele,' I said. 'God, why do you tolerate these jerks?'

'Because they talk all day and buy drinks all day. As long as they keep buying, I'll tolerate whoever the hell comes through that door.'

'Oh, really, and does that include me?'

'Aw, the pathetic drunk,' she said leaning close, her lips close to my own. I was getting a hard on. Damn, she was sexy. The room seemed to spin. I felt different.

'You want to go upstairs?' I said.

'Maybe,' she teased, 'but I want a drink first. I got to catch up with you!'

She ordered for us both. She put her hand on my leg, close enough to cause mischief. My dick was iron hard. I was going to give it to her good.

'Slow down,' she said with a wicked smile. 'You're practically fucking me from that chair. There's plenty of time. We've got all night.'

'Right,' I said, taking a drink. If my dick got any bigger it was going to tear through my pants and impale her.

'Anyway,' she said, 'about your friend. I remember now.'

'Remember what? And he's not my friend!'

'Who it is he reminds me of.'

'Go on,' I said.

'He looks like a really skinny version of that actor, David Cross.'

I choked on my beer, spitting it across the bar. 'David Cross?' I repeated, almost dropping my bottle. 'Are you sure?'

'Yeah,' she said, 'but a really skinny version, obviously.'

I cursed, leapt from the bar stool and ran out into the street. Dave was nowhere to be seen.

And then it hit me.

'Dave is Cross's W-Day twin!' I said to myself. 'He has to be!'

No, that's impossible, Storm! It's just too coincidental, too orchestrated!

I walked back into the bar. Ding Dong looked puzzled. 'What is it? What's wrong? You shot out of here like your ass was on fire!'

'My God,' I exclaimed. 'This is amazing! Jesus, it's like *fate*!'

'What's like fate?' she said. 'Tommy Storm, what is going on, please?'

'Synchronicity – or is it Kismet? – or something, I don't know!'

Ding Dong looked at me. 'You want to come upstairs now?'

Chapter 14

Ding Dong was in the shower. I lay in bed. It was damp and smelt of sex. I gathered my thoughts.

Prendergast was up to something. I wasn't seeing the whole picture here. What was the deal with his daughter and Cross if Cross were gay? Why had she eloped? *Had* she eloped? Maybe she had run away from Prendergast himself? Why? And for me to break my own golden rule and trust myself with the identity of the client, something big had to be going down.

I reached for the bottle of scotch on the bedside cabinet. I took a hit.

My thoughts turned to Dave. Ding Dong thought he looked like David Cross, but that meant nothing. In a certain light I looked like my uncle Bob, but I wasn't Bob. Then again, Ding Dong didn't look much like my aunt Jane, who at this point seemed little more than some irrelevant aside of a confused mind. I took another swig of scotch. I had made the connection because it was a convenient coincidence and I simply read too much into it. Dave just *happened* to look like a drugged-up, strung-out, fucked-up version of an actor who just *happened* to be involved in this case.

I felt better about this. The whole incident had given me a scare to be honest. I didn't like the idea of our lives being orches-trated in that way; that somebody else was moving the pieces and what you thought was a personal choice in fact belonged to a higher force. I took another drink. Things felt even better. And yet, there was a nasty nagging feeling in my gut that told me otherwise. I tried to ignore it.

Ding Dong stepped into the room, naked, ebony, slick-wet and beautiful. Man, I thought, she looks divine. A man could worship at a temple like that. She caught sight of me in the mirror looking at her. I saw her smile. It made me feel good.

'You know,' she said, applying moisturizer to her body, 'I like what we have.'

'I like it too,' I said.

'It's simple,' she continued, 'no bullshit between us. That's how I want to keep it.'

'Sounds good to me,' I said through yawning. I stretched. My back cricked loudly.

'Ouch!' winced Ding Dong.

I laughed. 'It does that from time to time. You cured me, thanks!'

She laughed. She had a good laugh. It was a laugh that made you feel free and easy. And for the moment, things felt fine.

As I swigged more scotch, the cell phone rang.

I tumbled out of bed, desperately searching for the phone. I found it in my trouser pocket. 'Hello?' I answered.

'It's me,' I replied.

'Okay, give me a second.' I pulled on my trousers and shirt and stepped out of the room into the corridor.

'Okay, what have you got for me?' I asked.

'I'm with Cross. We're coming to pick you up. Meet me at the office in a half hour.'

Chapter 15

I made my excuses and left Ding Dong, taking the bottle of scotch with me. As I left I hid it in my jacket but she savvied pretty quickly and demanded that I pick her up a bottle on the way back.

'You live over a bar!' I complained.

'Yeah, but it still *costs*, Tommy.'

'Fine, I'll pick you up a bottle on the way back.'

'I thought you were broke?' she called after me.

I stepped into the bar, pushing my way past the usual dross, headed for the door. I noticed Tom Rancher in the corner. He scowled at me. I gave him the finger.

Outside I heard a familiar voice behind me.

'Goddamn it, you just don't learn, do you?' It was the bartender I had fought the other night.

'You drink here? Listen, kid,' I said, holding up my hands, 'that birdie was for the asshole in the corner, not you.'

'That "asshole" just happens to be a very good friend of mine, you arrogant prick!'

Shit. I'd done it again. And the clock was ticking.

I had to run back to the office. My face was busted up. My left hand was bleeding. The kid had split my lip and cut my cheek. He'd beaten the living shit out of me, but he still lost. I bided my time until I could get a clear shot at his balls and then kicked out hard. He went down pissing his pants and crying for mama. I felt bad, so I left him a couple of bucks for beer before hotfooting it back to meet myself and Cross.

When I arrived at the office, there was nobody there. I checked my watch. I was twenty-three minutes late. I cursed and kicked the desk. I sat down, out of breath, my head pounding. I'd fucked it up big time. I was shit on God's heel for sure.

Sitting there in the dark, life felt useless. It seemed contrary to what should be, but what was that? I didn't know. I could barely think straight. All I knew was the taste of blood and booze in my mouth. My body stank of sex and sweat. My lungs felt polluted by the dirty breath of all the Tom Ranchers of this world. My eyes soiled by the likes of Prendergast. It was a lousy, no good world.

Chapter 16

Abandoning the office, I walked for a while. I figured I was making my way back to Ding Dong's, so I stopped off for a bottle of scotch. It was a warm evening. Night was falling to conceal my shame. Thank Christ for small mercies. Two women, hardly clothed, came towards me. One pointed at her friend and shouted, 'You want to fuck her?' Her friend screamed with laughter.

'Let me think about it,' I said, forcing a laugh as I passed, but I was feeling far from fucking jovial.

'Nice hat,' she called back.

'Yeah, it's a Berkeley,' I said.

'Yeah, I know.'

'Have a good evening, ladies.'

'Fuck you!'

I arrived back at Ding Dong's and tried for a screw, but she wasn't having any of it.

'I just showered,' she said.

As a compromise I suggested we fuck in the shower, but no dice. Ding Dong was done, thank you kindly.

Instead I sat down on her bed to gather my thoughts and muster up some sense of esteem and courage in the face of it all. The bed still reeked of fucking. It was a stale smell. I wished I was back in that bed with Ding Dong humping her ass all over again.

The cell phone buzzed into life. It was a message. The message read:

02.13.07

I checked for the number of the phone that sent the message, but there was none listed.

I sent a message back, saying:

WHO IS THIS?

The reply shot back almost instantly.

VALIS

Chapter 17

VALIS – acronym for Vast Active Living Intelligence System. It was the title of a book by an author called Philip K. Dick. I knew this because I had read it years ago. It was given to me by an old flame. She left me for a guy called Joe. From what I could remember, the book was about a guy who goes crazy and thinks he's two people whilst looking for the Messiah.

02.13.07 was the date I manifested my twin. It was W-Day. The connection was as sweet and clear as angel piss. Whoever sent this message had found a common link between what had happened to me on "W-Day" and a book I'd read over twenty years ago, that had all but vanished from my mind.

Two things went through my head:

That's impossible
Am I crazy?

Now I'm not the paranoid type, but this sent more than a few shivers down my spine. My stomach turned. I felt ill and began to retch. It felt like some sadistic bastard was applying a razor to my mind.

'Not on the carpet!' I heard Ding Dong shout in a panic.

I heaved myself off the bed and staggered into the bathroom. I spewed into the sink.

'Aw, shit! Tommy!'

I lurched over to the toilet and hung over the pan and retched and spewed. I vomited up all the booze. My body felt like it was on fire. I sweated like a son-of-a-bitch, still spewing, still retching and hacking. There was even blood in the mix.

'Christ,' said Ding Dong, closing the door in disgust, 'use the air freshener when you're done!'

I groaned a reply, sagging onto the floor, gasping for breath.

The lousy bathroom light looked like a million exploding suns, it was so fucking bright. I closed my eyes tight and rolled over, the brown nylon carpet tiles snagging at my stubble.

I lay there for a time. The inside of my head rolled over old memories; old girlfriends, scams I'd pulled, forgotten cases, my first kiss, my first whore, past friends and broken promises. Upon reflection, I truly was a bastard, but I didn't know how else to be. I hoped that it was a way to survive this cruel world and that it had some deep, inherent meaning. To think otherwise would have been enough to make me believe in sin.

The cell phone rang.

I left it.

It stopped ringing. That was much better.

Then it started ringing again.

I answered.

'Tommy?'

It was me again. 'Yeah,' I said, weakly.

'Are you okay? You don't sound so hot. Where are you?'

'At Ding Dong's,' I muttered, my eyes closing. 'I missed you. Sorry.'

'You didn't miss us. We never made it to the office. We were being tailed. We had to lose him.'

My eyes snapped open. 'Lose who?'

'It's a long story and we've not much time. I'll explain it later. Can you get up to the Cattle Club on Santa Monica?'

'Wait, isn't that a gay club?'

'That's right. Go to the VIP entrance and tell security Dino is waiting for you.'

'Jesus, as long as it's not the back-door entrance!' I cracked.

The phone went dead.

Chapter 18

There was only one way to decide if I was mad or not. I had to call Prendergast. I remembered he had said something about a friend of his with the same condition. I used the cell phone to call Prendergast. I was in a genuine panic here. I was sweating like a bastard, my hands trembled and I felt the urge to puke again.

Prendergast himself answered. 'Hello?'

'Prendergast,' I blurted, 'I need to ask you something!'

'Mister Storm? Is that you?'

'Yeah, yeah it's me. I'm sorry about the hour, but I need to know something. You said you had a friend with the same condition as me. Is that right?'

There was a long pause, then, 'Yes, that's correct.'

'Who is it?'

'Is this really necessary?' asked Prendergast, coldly.

'I'm afraid so,' I said, stammering out the words, 'if you want me to find your daughter then yes.'

Prendergast sighed. He sighed deeply. It sounded cautious and as though this entire conversation was against his better judgment.

'Please,' I begged.

'Very well,' said Prendergast. 'It's my daughter's lover, the actor, David Cross.'

Without another word I hung up.

I couldn't believe it. My mind just collapsed and went numb, and then *slowly* the realizations dawned: Dave really was Cross' twin. I just *knew* it.

And I knew, with the same profound depth of absolute certainty, that 02.13.07 and VALIS was a message from the same source.

I wasn't mad. It was worse. Somebody else *was* moving the pieces. Some higher force *was* pulling the strings. And whoever the hell it was, they knew both the case and they sure as hell knew *me*. And that really pissed me off. It was time to get busy. It was time to go to work.

Dave never showed up at Ding Dong's. By the time I staggered out to head over to Dino's it was way past ten. There had been no sign of that loopy tit-obsessed fucker all night.

Luckily for me it was ladies night at the Cattle Club. Lesbians as far as the eye could see. The music was loud, the women were hot and so was I. As security led me through the club I had to excuse myself and go to the bathroom and quickly jerk off in one of the stalls. Sometimes a man needs relief from such things in order to concentrate on the task at hand. And I needed to be focused.

Dino was waiting for me in the farthest corner of the VIP lounge. He looked like a cross between George Hamilton and a gimp.

'Mr Storm,' he said, gesturing my ass to the chair next to his.

I sat down. I kept looking at the lesbians. Two were kissing right in my line of vision. They were hot, well-stacked, beautiful and horny. It was all slow tongue between them. So much for keeping focused.

'Mr Storm?'

'Oh, yeah, hi,' I said, clearing my throat. 'You're Dino, I take it?'

He looked puzzled. 'Sorry, the music is *very* loud in here tonight. Did you just say that I'm Dino and that *you take it*?'

'No, I'm afraid not.'

'I thought you were hitting on me.'

'No.'

'Oh,' said Dino, and he took a drink of wine. 'Okay, listen I received a phone call from a very good friend of mine. I think you know him? David?'

'David Cross,' I affirmed.

Dino put a finger to my lips. 'Not so loud, please! Discretion,

Mr Storm! I have been asked to ensure your safe delivery to a location where David is waiting for you. My driver will take you.'

I leaned close. 'Sorry, the music is very loud in here tonight. Did you just say that your driver will take me?'

Dino caressed my face with his finger. 'Hush, dear. There's a limo waiting for you outside, so get your sweet ass into it!'

And with that, I was gone.

Chapter 19

Dino's car was a plush affair – leather interior with air condi-tioning, a bar, satellite navigation, cable access, stereo and even a change of clothes. I helped myself to the bar. The driver caught a glance of me in the mirror.

'Dino said I could,' I lied, pouring myself a large scotch.

I felt good. Well, better. I wasn't mad, or in the very least no crazier than every other mad prick in this city. I was on a roll and finally going to get some answers. Just what the hell was going on? And what had become of Dave? And why did I even care? I shrugged it off. Why suffer fish shit when you can have caviar? I was going to see the real deal: Dave Cross, film star, in the flesh. And the lovely Rochelle, come to think of it.

The more I thought about it, the more I realized that I was no longer looking for Rochelle Prendergast; I was looking for Dave Cross. That's all Prendergast himself really cared about at the end of the day. His precious film, *The Dark Mind*, and how negative publicity might affect box-office returns. What a shit-kicker!

It began to rain. Huge spats hit the windows of the car and drummed hard upon the rooftop. There was a quick flash of lightning, followed by a hungry growl of thunder. It continued this way for about an hour as we drove west and out towards Venice.

Upon arriving in Venice the limo cruised down the front towards the pier. I could see the big wheel turning. It reminded me of the time I lost $16,000 playing roulette in Vegas, the fucker.

The driver pulled up outside The Sandpiper hotel. He wasted no time in getting my scotch-stealing ass out of the car and into the lobby.

After I checked-in, the limo driver handed me an envelope then left without a word. I checked the envelope. Inside was a key.

'Mr. Storm,' said the receptionist, who was all teeth and no tits, 'you'll be staying in room seven, second floor.'

'Thanks,' I said. 'Is the bar still open?'

'I'm afraid not, but there's a mini-bar in the room.'

I nodded, collected the key card and made my way up the stairs to the second floor. I found room seven and in I went. The room was pretty. It had a nice double bed, en suite, mini bar and cable. Pretty, but not great. Still, it was free. I hoped. I noticed a clean suit hanging from the wardrobe. It was my size. Pinned to it was a note, saying:

FOR MR THOMAS STORM

'Shit,' I said. It was a pretty expensive suit. It even matched the Berkeley. I was impressed. I decided to shower and crawl into bed and empty the mini-bar. Maybe there was some good porn showing?

I lay in bed, drunk, watching *Fuck Sluts IV* and unable to get it up. It was three in the morning. Slowly, I drifted off. The television stayed on and I was awoken by the agonized cries of a girl getting it up the ass by three guys wearing ski goggles singing *Edelweiss*. I turned the set off and rolled onto my side. I felt beyond exhaustion. I felt the sense of a knot being untied and of release in some way. I couldn't explain it. Then again, I couldn't explain a lot of things that had happened of late.

Chapter 20

I awoke at seven the following morning. I was not alone.

Standing at the foot of my bed was a woman. She was tall and blonde, with full lips and piercing blue almond-shaped eyes. She was dressed in a white cotton dress. I could make out her figure in the light. She was shapely in all the right places.

'Mr Storm,' she said in a voice of delicate porcelain, 'my name is Rochelle Prendergast.'

I said nothing for a few moments. There was something strange about this woman. Her voice seemed to penetrate me to my core, the words and intonations piercing my soul and wrapping about my heart and mind. All the worries of a lifetime felt subdued. I felt nothing but peace. It was a struggle even to speak.

'Hey,' I managed.

She smiled. It felt as if I was falling in love with her anew every time she moved. She blinked, and I felt a rush of love. She opened her mouth to speak and I felt love. She took a step closer and the love exploded through my body again. In the end I gasped, 'Please stop!' I thought it was going to kill me.

'I understand,' she said. 'It will pass, though. You'll get accustomed to it, trust me.'

The love was now feeling unrequited. A painful yearning for something – or somebody – I could never have. I'd not felt this way since I was a teenager. 'God damn it, this is fucking weird!'

Rochelle laughed. 'Maybe I can help,' and she stepped forward and sat on the bed next to me.

I looked into her eyes and without thinking twice I said, 'I love you.'

She leaned forward and kissed me. I felt the room spin. Pain shot though my body. It felt as if my skin had been peeled away and every nerve was flinching to the air with raw exposure. She kissed me good. She slipped her tongue into my mouth. I greedily pushed mine in between those lips and held her close. I wanted to fuck her there on the bed. I was iron hard and ready. I began feeling her tits and fingering a nipple through the cotton dress.

And then I opened my eyes.

She was still standing, as before, at the foot of the bed and smiling.

'Hey, wait a second,' I said.

She laughed loudly, quickly putting her hand to her mouth. 'I'm sorry, forgive me!'

'What the hell just happened there?'

'Feeling better?'

I realized that I was indeed feeling better. 'Yeah, but...'

'Don't worry about it,' she said, 'a little trick of mine. I'll explain everything later. You want breakfast?'

Chapter 21

After breakfast we walked on the beach, down by the surf. I couldn't take my eyes off her. She was perfect in every way. Over breakfast we'd made small talk. Well, I'd made small talk, she just talked about anything and everything under the sun; how good the grapefruit was, wasn't the coffee delicious but not as good as papa Prendergast had back home, last night the sunset reminded her of a painting she'd seen years ago but couldn't remember the name of, what she liked best about L.A., the guy sitting at the table opposite reminded her of her high-school math teacher; it was endless. As though she were a constant source of information backed up and ready to be applied to the minute detail of her life. Everything had a story.

And now, on the beach, she was quiet. She just looked out over the ocean, off towards the horizon, lost in her own private world. And I looked at her, not the ocean, not out towards the unknown, but at what I could see in front of me. Even the experience in the hotel room didn't seem to matter a damn. She fascinated me on some level hitherto untouched by any woman before or since.

I just hoped she didn't notice my hard-on. It was pretty much poking out and no matter how hard I tried, the damn thing refused to go down.

'So,' I began, 'what's going on here, Miss Prendergast?'

'Let's take it easy,' she replied. 'Your W-Day twin, David Cross and I, decided that I should be the one to inform you of the situation. However, the *situation* is going to be hard for you to believe.'

'Try me,' I said, stooping down for a shell. It was white and pink.

'Not yet,' she said, and reached out to take my hand. 'Let's just walk awhile. It's beautiful today. Everything just feels new.'

I looked around. 'It just looks the same to me' I said.

Rochelle laughed and squeezed my hand. 'Don't be such a grump,' she said, 'and don't sulk. It doesn't do anything for you. You'll find out everything soon enough, Tommy Storm, I swear. Just enjoy the moment.'

We walked on in silence.

After a time she said, 'Let me buy you a hat. I know a great place that sells hats. You need a trilby.'

'I like my hat,' I said. 'It's a Berkeley.'

'Yeah, I know, and it's okay, but a little *tatty*, don't you think?'

'Just like its owner,' I said, smiling.

'C'mon, would you? Let me buy you a trilby. You don't have to wear it if you don't want, just consider it a gift.'

'Okay,' I said, thinking, *this is crazy*. It was like being out on a date. And I'd never been out with any woman as beautiful as this. Men actually stopped and stared at her. They slowed down and turned their heads as we passed. I felt like the luckiest son-of-a-bitch alive. The amazing thing was she put all of her time and her attention into *me*. I had to keep reminding myself we weren't a couple and that I had been hired to find her.

Chapter 22

Hats Entertainment! was owned by a large, dope smoking slack ass called Dando. His shop was situated next door to the pipe shop. The owner of that shop knew him very well.

'Yeah, he's out back, the fat fucking prick,' said Carlos, rearranging his bongs. 'I'll go get him for you.'

'Thanks,' said Rochelle, holding onto my arm. 'You're gonna get a brand new hat!' she whispered excitedly in my ear.

My hard-on went into overdrive.

'Hey, hi, how are you this fine day?' said Dando shuffling towards us, his long goatee caught by the breeze. 'My name is Dando, I own this fine boutique to all things...' he lost the word, 'hats?' he guessed.

'Hi, Dando, I'm looking for a real sexy trilby for my friend here.'

'Let me see, let me see...' Dando muttered, perusing the hats.

'There it is! That's the one!' said Rochelle, practically jumping for joy. 'There on the stand by the counter!'

She released my arm and walked past Dando, over to the stand by the counter and retrieved the trilby.

'Good choice,' said Dando. 'Nice hat.'

'As if you'd know,' I heard Carlos say. 'Shithead.'

'Spick,' coughed Dando into his hand, before vanishing from sight into the shop to serve Rochelle.

'Hey, what was that? Did that motherfucker just call me a spick?'

'No, you misheard,' I said.

'Oh, really,' Carlos said. 'And what did I *mishear* exactly?'

'He didn't call you a spick,' I assured Carlos.

'Good.'

'More like "cunt", unless *I* misheard.'

I got a mouthful in Spanish and Carlos walked away.

Another ethnic group offended by my smart mouth. Still, it was cheering to know I wasn't prejudiced in my assaults. Every creed and nation was a target.

'Got it,' said Rochelle, bounding towards me with an enthusiasm I would have associated with a horny cheerleader. 'Put it on!'

I looked at the black, velvet trilby. It just wasn't me.

'Please,' Rochelle said, 'just give it a go.'

I removed the Berkeley and Rochelle immediately snatched it away and put it on her own head. 'Mine now. Now you have to wear the trilby!'

I forced a smile and on went the trilby.

'Take a look in the mirror,' she suggested.

'You look like a faggot!' yelled Carlos.

'Shut up, you dumb spick!' bellowed Dando from inside the shop.

'Motherfucker, I knew you called me a spick!'

'Try this on for size, you're also an asshole!'

'Screw you! I'm calling the cops! I'm sick of your shit!'

'Ignore them,' said Rochelle, quietly. 'What do you think?'

I was lost for a moment in her eyes, and then I took a look in the mirror. I adjusted the hat. I took it off and then put it back on a few times, getting the feel for it.

Rochelle watched me, her smile growing.

'It's great,' I said finally, smiling. 'It's me.'

'Not yet,' she said, 'but we're getting there.'

Chapter 23

We walked back to the hotel for lunch.

'I'm in the mood for a steak,' said Rochelle. 'You like steak?'

'I love steak.'

'Well-cooked?'

'Medium,' I corrected, 'with a red wine.'

'Medium-cooked with a glass of red wine it is,' she announced, taking my arm.

All through lunch, the questions were mounting up. One especially was creeping to the fore of my mind: was it all a set-up? Was this all part of a game? Could I actually trust this woman? My gut said 'no', but south of that wasn't hearing too well. It was time for some answers.

'Rochelle,' I said firmly, 'I think we need to talk about why I'm here.'

'I agree,' said Rochelle, 'but finish your steak first and then go up to your room and change into the suit David left you. Do that and then we can begin, I promise you.'

'Begin what?'

She looked into my eyes. 'Don't fret so, Storm. I won't bite.'

'Shame,' I said, stuffing a chunk of steak into my mouth.

Rochelle gave me a knowing smile.

She came up to the room with me. She held my hand all the way. It was warm and soft. I stroked the skin of her hand with my thumb and she returned the affection.

Stop this, I chided myself, *this is stupid! It's madness! This does not happen. Not to you at least. It's a trick, be careful Storm! You're walking straight into a trap here!*

We arrived at room seven. My heart did summersaults in my chest. I felt light-headed. At first I thought it could be the wine, but I knew it was her. She was doing this to me. She made me feel young again, plain and simple. As if the world lay *before* me, and not in the past.

Inside my room, she took the suit from out of the wardrobe and laid it on the bed. I stood there, watching her, not daring to move or to break the spell. She moved close to me.

'Let's begin,' she said in a whisper, and began to remove my clothes.

I wanted to lean in and kiss her, but I couldn't. I was being held fast by her eyes. She just stared at me, without blinking, as she removed my jacket and then began to unbuckle my belt. I grabbed her by the wrist and pulled her closer.

'Are you fucking with me?' I demanded, angrily.

She blinked and smiled. 'No, Tommy, but I'm not going to fuck you either. So, please let go.'

I got pissed off and stepped back, releasing her wrist. 'What is this, a game? What the fuck is going on here, Prendergast? Tell me!'

'Put the suit on,' she replied softly. 'Here, let me help.'

She slipped the jacket on over my shoulders. Then she unbuckled my belt and stepped back.

'You can take it from there, big boy,' she said, 'I'll fix us a drink.'

I grabbed the suit trousers and vanished into the bathroom. Whilst in there I thought *what the fuck* and jerked off. It didn't take long and Christ knows I needed it.

'Are you okay, Tommy?'

'Fine,' I said, dropping the used toilet paper down the shitter. 'I'll be there in a second.'

I finished dressing and sat down on the toilet to gather myself together. I was thinking of Ding Dong. I missed her, and yet given half the chance I'd fuck this Prendergast prick tease in a heartbeat. What the fuck was wrong with me? Ding Dong didn't care. Who cared if I fucked Rochelle? What was I even thinking this shit for?

I stepped out of the bathroom. Rochelle was sitting on the bed, a glass of scotch in each hand. 'We'll both need these,' she said offering one towards me.

'Thanks,' I said and took the glass.

She sat on the bed. 'Sit next to me, Tommy.'

'I'd rather not.'

'Sit down,' she said, shifting up slightly to make room for me. 'Please?'

I sat next to her. My dick stirred. My balls ached. My heart was singing opera.

'Okay,' Rochelle began, 'where to start. You ask away. I'm all yours, so to speak.'

'Fine,' I snapped, 'let's start with just that, shall we? Why the prick tease act? I mean, you getting off on this little escapade, sweetheart? Is this what you do for kicks?'

She sighed. 'Look in the mirror. What do you see, Tommy?'

I looked. I told her what I saw. 'I see me. I see you. Is that it?'

'Look at yourself. What do you see?'

'Christ! I see me in a suit I could never afford, how about that?'

'You know what I see?'

'What?'

'I see a man wearing a suit he could never afford, but is wearing it anyway.'

I looked at her. 'I don't follow.'

'No,' she said, 'you won't, not yet, but someday you will. In the meantime please accept this suit as a gift, along with the trilby.'

And with that she leaned over and kissed me.

'You want to make love, now?'

'No,' I said.

She smiled. 'That's better. I think we can get down to business now. The problem is, I don't know how to begin,' she said, 'but it's probably best if we start on something you already experienced. When you woke up this morning, you ever stop to consider how I got into your room? How I did my little trick?'

'It was the last thing on my mind at the time,' I laughed.

She smiled. 'Have you ever heard of The Dark Mind?'

'The film your father is working on,' I replied.

'No, not that,' she said. 'The Dark Mind is a philosophical notion...' she chose her words again, more carefully, '...actually more of a *spiritual* notion. An experience, a state of...' the thought escaped her again. 'Shit, this is harder than I thought!'

'It's fine,' I said, taking her hand, 'we have plenty of time.'

She said nothing for a time and then reached into her bag and pulled out an envelope. She handed it to me.

'You'd best read this,' Rochelle said, 'I'll meet you downstairs when you're done.'

'What is it?'

She got up off the bed, slipped on her shoes and made for the door. 'It's a starting point. That's all. The truth is far stranger, Tommy. Please read it carefully. It's the key to everything.'

She opened the door to leave. She looked troubled.

'Tommy, change of plan. Read it and wait for me here. I'll come pick you up either later this afternoon, this evening or first thing tomorrow morning. Either way I'll let you know.'

'Okay,' I said, leaning back and opening the envelope.

Inside was something both remarkable and disturbing. Note upon note of scribbled thoughts, hurriedly taken down on various paper scraps. Whoever wrote this was sure in a hurry to get these thoughts down. I skimmed through the notes. I recognized the handwriting. It was my own. I began to read.

Two minds: one light and one dark. The darker mind is the believer and maker of the illusion of the world. The lighter mind is trapped by the mind of darkness. If you can see the darker mind – separate the two – he is on the run. He is scared of the lighter self. He just wants the veil of normality – of the man-made world – to exist and nothing more.

We must conquer the material world. It is a trap and an illusion.

The darker self is not evil, but it is controlling. Its grip is very weak, hence it must bind the lighter self in delusions that take precedence, weakening the lighter self and giving all power to the darker self.

I saw the Dark Mind personified, casting nets and making traps with thoughts and images. He was in shadow, maneuvering the components of the illusory self – the ego – in order to stay in control and be dominant. I saw him and I knew that he was aware of being exposed for the first time. He was desperate to be hidden again and began to attempt to shift my attention into the prison of 'self'.

I know that the Dark Mind is the warden of the prison, but his power is not all encompassing. Once seen, once glimpsed, his power began to weaken and I could see that he bound and chained up the Light Mind so as to be blind, dumb, suffocated and less than alive. A true prisoner: no liberty. No right to thrive in the world. And yet the Dark Mind's power, his control, was as illusory as the 'self' and ego.

The Dark Mind is not evil. It is simply a false construct, ever working as a false creator, architect and design and construction all in one.

It is the Demiurge of Gnostic truth.

Every prisoner goes from day to day doing everything required of them in order to survive – survive within the design laid out by every other Dark Mind that has existed down through history, following the same pattern and making the prison walls thick and impenetrable. Society, money, trade, pleasure, vice and all distractions are the building blocks of the prison.

Was the imprisonment by design or merely a by-product of an evolving species?

The 'Dark Mind' never tires.

I've not broken down, I've broken free.

And there I stopped reading. The rest was incomprehensible to my tired mind. I took a drink and paced the room, lost in thought. The cell phone suddenly sprang into life. It was Rochelle.

'Tommy, I'll pick you up tomorrow morning at seven. The driver gave you a key, I hope. Bring it with you, you'll need it.'

Chapter 24

I hit the sack early, but woke up just after midnight. My head was swimming, thick and muggy. My body ached and I needed a piss. I hauled my ass out of the bed and trouped to the bathroom. I didn't turn on the light. I just pissed in the dark with the door open. I missed the pan a couple of times but didn't care. I just wanted to get back into bed and sleep. I didn't even bother to flush.

The alarm sounded at six-thirty. The 'thickness' in my head remained. No doubt some smart ass would say, 'Hell, Tommy, that's natural for you', but this was different. I felt sick. Real sick and was sweating like a pedophile in a nursery.

I staggered into the bathroom and dropped to my knees. I vomited into the toilet. I could smell urine in the water, mixing with the odious smell of my own puke. I retched and spewed some more. I was vaguely aware of kneeling in my own cold piss. Jesus, could I get any lower than this? Today was the day, the big day, the day when all the answers came and I could mentally reinstate myself as a private dick of some credibility and worth. Instead I was surrounded by puke and piss, all of it my own. I guess that, at least, was a small mercy.

'Must have been that goddamn steak,' I told myself, groaning as another load came up, 'Sweet bastard!'

After about ten minutes of this sorry display I stopped heaving, had a shower, shaved and then dressed. I felt a little better, but not by much.

There was a knock at the door.

'Who is it?'

'Rochelle Prendergast, Tommy. Remember?'

'Yeah, I remember,' I muttered under my breath. Who in the hell could forget?

'I'll wait down in the lobby, then?'

'Yeah,' I called, 'I'll be there in five minutes.'

'Shut up you inconsiderate assholes!' I heard a voice call from the room next door. 'I'm trying to sleep!'

'Up yours, buddy!' I hollered back. 'And mind your own goddamn business!'

'Did he just call me an asshole?' I heard the voice ask.

'Yeah, he did! The bastard! Go kick his ass, Joe!'

I heard a heavy man leap out of bed. The floor shook. I could hear him pulling on his clothes, cursing with a vengeance.

'Fuck this,' I said, and made for the door. As I slipped out the door to room six opened and out stepped a huge brute of a man. He was built like a tank. A tank matted with sprawling body hair and body odor. My ass was dead.

'Holy shit, I don't believe it!'

'What?' I said, looking behind me.

'Christ, Sandra, look who it is!'

Sandra emerged from the room. 'Jesus, Tommy! Tommy Storm! How the hell are you?'

Sandra was the old flame who had given me the copy of VALIS all those years ago and left me for a guy named Joe. I always wondered what Joe looked like. Turned out it was Joe Kaplan. He was a lecturer at the college where I met Sandra.

'You still look the same,' he said, smiling and putting a hand on my shoulder.

I nodded. 'You still have my girl.' And I jabbed my knee into his ball sack.

I then reliably informed Sandra she was a back-stabbing bitch, and that her unwashed pussy stank from the collected semen of the nations she had fucked behind my back at college.

'*You* cheated on *me*, you shit!' Sandra spat back. 'I moved on!'

I deflected her clever attempt to use the truth against me by saying nothing. Then I turned and walked away, leaving Joe holding his balls and Sandra hurling abuse at me down the corridor as I descended the stairs, down into the lobby.

'Tommy, are you okay?' asked Rochelle. 'You look a little spooked.'

I laughed. 'Spooked? You have no idea. Okay, where's this party at?'

'What party?'

I seized the moment. 'It's a figure of speech, you know, a turn of phrase?'

'God, please *don't* say that,' she grimaced, 'my father says that *all* the time. Come on, big boy, there's a car outside.'

Chapter 25

We headed south for about a half hour, maybe forty-five minutes. Conversation ran from tedious to plain dull. Rochelle was not her usual self today. She seemed dead inside. When I asked her if there was something wrong, she just said, 'I'm tired,' and that was that. Eventually we arrived at a large construction site. By all accounts it looked abandoned.

'Okay, we're here,' she said. 'Let's go.'

'Go where?'

'In there,' and she pointed towards the locked gates of the site.

'How do we get in?'

'God, Tommy! I have a key. We unlock the gate and we go in, okay?'

'Okay,' I said.

Rochelle sighed. Her breasts looked great when she sighed. I should have offered her some sort of a shoulder to cry on, allow her to spill the beans on what was bothering her, but I was lost in those juicy mounds of flesh. They were truly amazing. God, I wanted to fuck her. Maybe fuck her tits? I think they call it a 'French salad' in Europe. I wasn't sure, but…

'Jesus, are you looking at my tits?'

'What? No! I was thinking. I just zoned out.'

'Yeah, thinking about my tits, probably.'

'Jesus, what is wrong with you today? I mean, yesterday you were all over me like a rash, but today!'

Rochelle lowered her head and sighed again. 'Tommy, this is difficult, but I…' she looked up, catching my gaze. 'Fuck, you're doing it again!'

'Rochelle,' I snapped, 'I was *not* looking at your tits, okay? And quite frankly, I'm getting a little pissed off with these accusations and finger pointing. What, you *want me* to look at your tits? Here!'

I leaned in and took a real good look.

Rochelle put her hand over her cleavage, 'No! Look, I'm sorry, okay? I'm truly sorry. It's just that most guys only ever talk to my fucking tits, you know? It really gets me down. Just promise me you won't be like the others, Tommy, okay?'

I nodded. 'I promise.'

She nodded, taking a few moments to cool down. 'Okay, let's go.'

She got out of the car and I stole a good look at her ass. God, she was sexy. Her ass looked like a ripe peach and my dick was the knife to dig out that deep set stone. Oh, baby!

Rochelle unlocked the gate and I stepped through. It was indeed abandoned and desolate.

'It was originally planned as an exclusive art-house multiplex,' Rochelle informed me.

'What happened?'

She shrugged. 'I don't know for sure. Money dried up. I think this was one of the projects 'Prize Horse Pictures' had on the boil before they went down. My father was attached at some point. He was helping to raise money to save the multiplex, or something. Christ knows why. It's just another one of his pointless projects, where he calls in favors for fuck all and ends up with nothing.'

The skeletal frame of the multiplex, the huge stone blocks, dust-covered and bone dry, reminded me of some vast artistic cadaver. It made me feel good. As it was, the site was a million times better than the piece of shit that would have stood in its place. If only every goddamn cinema in this shit pit land of industry would go the same way.

We arrived at some concrete steps leading down into the earth. It looked like the entrance to the grave. Rochelle went first. I followed. My eyes followed her ass. 'What a way to go,' I thought, a smile creeping over my face.

'This would have been the basement,' said Rochelle, 'or

maybe not. I don't know. Either way, they're all down here. Did you bring the key?'

'I most certainly did.'

'Good. It's important.' She flicked a switch and some crude, rudimentary lights glowed in the dark. 'The door at the end, just go through. They're in there.'

'Aren't you coming?'

'I hate it down here. I'm claustrophobic. See you later, big boy.'

'See you later.'

And she ascended up into the light, leaving me alone in the gloom of the underworld.

I walked the length of the corridor slowly. Each step took me closer to the truth. I was savoring the moment. I had earned this. I deserved it, frankly. I was Tommy Storm, private investigator, back on form and doing what I did best. Which, of course was pure horse shit, but it sounded good for the moment. No, for *this* moment: the moment of truth. I opened the door, allowing it to swing wide for the big reveal.

Chapter 26

And there I was, sitting on a chair, reading the paper. I didn't even bother to look up when I said, 'Nice entrance.'

'Where's Cross?'

'He's busy. You want a drink?'

'What have you got?'

'We have coffee.'

'Is that all?'

'I'm afraid so.' I gestured to the coffee pot. 'Knock yourself out.'

I wandered over and poured myself a cup. 'You want one?' I asked.

'I'm fine, thanks.'

I poured myself a cup. It was old and – if brown had a taste – this was it.

'Have a seat,' I said, 'there's some chairs behind the door. Not the wicker one. It's broken.'

I grabbed a small wooden chair that was painted blue. I placed it opposite me and sat down.

'What happened to your hand?' I asked, glancing up from the paper.

'Never mind,' I said, getting down to business, 'let's talk. What the hell is going on here, Tommy?'

I folded the paper, fixed me dead in the eye and said, 'The Dark Mind. That's what's going on, Tommy. The question is, are you ready to see it?'

I drank the cup of brown. 'I read your notes.'

'And..?'

I took a few moments, and then said, 'I think you've lost your fucking mind. I think you should head back to Hollywood, back to the office and let me handle this.'

I shook my head and laughed. 'I'm not mad, Tommy.'

'No?'

'No,' I said calmly, 'if anybody is, it's you.'

I looked myself in the eye. I looked deep. I wasn't kidding. 'Do tell,' I prompted.

'I saw the Dark Mind, Tommy. It had your face.'

This sent a chill through me. I played it casual. 'Are you sure it wasn't Uncle Sol? You know how we look so alike.'

I didn't laugh. 'I'm serious, Tommy. You are the Dark Mind.'

'And what the fuck are you, if you don't mind my asking?'

'I'm awake.'

'Maybe, maybe not,' I said. 'How do you know that I'm not the one who is awake and you're the fucked-up dreamer here?'

I smiled at that one, and so did I.

'Good question,' I said. 'You have the key?'

I nodded.

'Then go through there,' I pointed to a small wooden door at the far end of the room, 'and know for sure.'

I rose to my feet and walked over to the door. It looked like any other door. I inserted the key into the lock and turned. It unlocked.

I opened the door and stepped inside.

The best way to describe what happened next is to be honest and say that I can't. I couldn't handle it, at first. I turned away, falling to my knees, my mind unable to cope with what I saw. I thought I was going insane.

It was like a multitude of mirrors, with each surface reflecting what seemed like infinity right back at you, and yet each mirror – or lens – not occupying the same time or space. It wasn't even a collection of mirrors. That's just what it was *like*, but the truth is, the more I think on it, the less I want to be able to comprehend it. To bring it up into my mind as I first saw it might drive me crazy. I'd end up as cracked as the asshole that sent me into the room. Music began playing. Loud, 1940's music that crackled and popped upon an unseen gramophone.

'This is the Prismatic Moderator!' sang a reedy voice from the recording. 'You will notice there is nothing up its sleeves, for it does not have any sleeves!'

The recording instantly crawled to a slow drag, and then silence.

The most disturbing thing about the Prismatic Moderator was its sense of life as nothing but information to be processed. That was the worst thing. You got that instantly and in spades. You were a bit, a pixel, a counting bean, an equation or at least part of one. And you didn't mean shit. Everything you thought important, life and love, was meaningless to the cold bastard. It didn't even really care about the Dark Mind or the collapse of the Light Mind. It just wasn't interested. It just processed the information.

'The twin,' said the Moderator, after a time. 'You got the information I sent to you?'

The word VALIS and then 02.13.07 entered my mind.

The Moderator continued, 'Does this prove my reach?'

'Yes,' I said, not really knowing what I was saying.

'It was important to verify *this* present moment, *back then*. Do you understand?'

I shook my head. 'No, I don't understand.'

'You made a connection between the book and the W-Day event that you successfully proved to be, at best, tenuous. The point was to verify that I know you. That I could reach back and take forgotten memories and unforgettable events and marry the two in order to prove my reach. I also chose the information to fit about the running program so as to induce what you might call a coincidence.'

'Dave?'

'And at the hotel,' said the Moderator.

I thought for a few moments and then realized, 'Joe and Sandra.'

'Correct.'

'You manipulate people?'

'I process data, Twin. I am the Prismatic Moderator. With every universe that comes into being, so do I to process all information – laws and life, great and small.'

I kept my gaze on the floor, heaving in the presence of such power.

'I shall keep this short, Thomas,' said the Moderator. 'Your twin spoke to you about the Dark Mind. You also read his Gospel – the notes of his revelation. Do you understand what the Dark Mind is?'

'I think so,' I gasped, my hands blocking the brilliance of fire and light emitting from the life-form before me.

'Explain it to me.'

I could hardly think straight. I wanted to look up but was scared that my mind might break. 'According to what I read, it's everything. It's society. It's money and work, and drink and sports and paying our taxes and buying shit we don't need. Stuff like that, right?'

'The Dark Mind is a prison. All that you see belongs to the bars of this prison. The question is: how was the prison built? Who allowed it to take hold and who laid the foundation stone?'

'I don't know.'

The Prismatic Moderator flexed, growing closer to me. It uttered the answer in what should have been a whisper, but the word cut me to the quick, shaking my soul into a place of such intense fear that I felt the need to run, to escape and be done with this madness.

The answer was 'Prendergast.'

Chapter 27

'Now do you believe?' it asked.

'Prendergast created the Dark Mind?'

'Yes,' said the Moderator, 'the Dark Mind is the prison he forged in ignorance. It has taken many lifetimes to achieve the power and strength it now holds. Prendergast is greedy, you see? And he knows, Thomas. Deep down, he knows all too well what has happened. Tell me, what is the title of his new film?'

'*The Dark Mind,*' I said. 'He had that statue in his garden.'

'Yes, and for good reason. Remember what he told you of that statue?'

Yes, I remembered. And the thought made me laugh. And then I stopped laughing. No, it wasn't funny.

The Moderator continued. 'Seduced by his own creation, he dips into the world of flesh and matter and loses himself.'

I shook my head. 'That's impossible!' I wasn't buying any of this.

'And every time the word becomes flesh, the Logos has to be set free in order to be returned to His rightful place.'

'What's a Logos?'

'It is Greek for "word". Reference the Gospel of John. "*In the beginning was the Word and the Word was with God and the Word was God.*" Try *reading* sometime. There's no shame in it.'

I buried my face into the dirt and began laughing again. This was madness.

'Divine seduction,' stated the Prismatic Moderator. 'He is obsessed by what achieves worshipfulness. As it is written in your Exodus; "*You shall bow down to no other god, for Yahweh's name is the Jealous One; he is a jealous God.*" Do you understand?'

Oh, I understood alright. Did I believe a word of it? No. Then again, did I really have a conversation with a higher being who knew me better than I knew myself, sending me information to verify this and every moment of doubt? I question it all to this very day.

'You do not believe in God, Thomas. You are the doubting twin. You will not believe unless you see, and even then you will question. That is why we need your help.'

I had a hunch as to what was coming.

'We need your help to release the Logos so as to restore the balance.'

I said nothing for a while, and then asked, 'Balance to *what*, exactly?'

'That is beyond you,' said the Moderator, 'all you need know is that the presence of the Demiurge is akin to a virus in the system. It is not a necessary part of the running loop of information. It impedes and corrupts.'

'The Dark Mind,' I said.

'Yes, the Dark Mind is the result of the Demiurge losing himself in his own vanity. He is enchanted and seduced by his own handiwork and forgets himself. As ignorant a god he is, he is still necessary. If he is not in his place, the information cannot flow. Entropy sets in. The program is rendered useless and aborts before its time. I was forced to double up on available information in order to inject new areas of potential flow and movement into the already corrupted information processing. W-Day, as you called it, was my doing. I cannot tell you anymore than this.'

And with that, I got the hell out of the room.

Chapter 28

'So?' I asked, still reading the paper.

I walked over to the blue chair and sat down. My head reeled. Tears were in my eyes. 'You bastard,' I said, trying to hold back the sobs.

'It happens to everyone, Tommy,' I said, turning the page, 'just let it out.'

I lunged forward and tore the paper from my hands and landed a blow to my face. I went sprawling to the floor. I put the boot in and made sure I got the message loud and clear.

'Enough!' said a voice behind me.

I turned around. There was David Cross. 'Enough,' he repeated.

I was furious, pissed off beyond measure, and I made a move for Cross. I wanted some answers and if I had to beat them out of the son-of-a-bitch, then so be it.

Cross pulled a gun and pointed it at me, his hand trembling. 'Stay back!'

I took a few good steps back.

'Way to go,' I said, holding a bleeding nose and rising to my feet.

'Fuck you,' I spat back. 'Fuck all of you!'

'Both of you sit down,' said Cross. 'From now on I'll do all the talking. You just listen, okay?'

'Put the gun down,' I said.

'Sit down,' repeated Cross, brandishing the piece. 'I mean it!'

We both sat down. I reached for my coffee. It was still on the floor by the side of the chair. I took a mouthful. It was cold.

'You have a tissue?' I asked me. I handed one over. 'Thanks' I said, applying it to my nose. Cross lowered the gun, breathing easy and wiping the sweat from his brow. 'I'm sorry about that,' he said, 'but this is too important to jeopardize with menial squabbling. The Dark Mind is ever present, it never rests. Every moment of every day it will do anything and everything to regain control. We must stay awake at all times.'

'Yes,' I said, wiping away the blood from my nose, 'I'm sorry. You're right.'

'Would somebody mind telling me what the fuck I just saw in there?' I ventured.

Cross looked at me and then at my twin. I turned to see me looking a little sheepish. 'He went in?' asked Cross.

'He wanted to know,' I responded.

'It should have been his choice, Tommy,' said Cross. 'It could have broken his mind.'

'I'm still waiting!' I cut in.

Cross was real nervous. He paced the room, gun in hand, sweating and edgy.

'That,' he began 'is the Prismatic Moderator. It is the system that processes the information of the entire universe. Every action, every choice, every thought is information, and the information is stored within its infinite memory. Of course, that is the Moderator for this universe. There are countless others, for the countless multiverses of creation.' Cross stopped pacing. 'Tommy, what did the Moderator tell you exactly?'

I sighed. 'That Prendergast is a God that has become trapped in this world, or something. And we have to set him free.'

'Yes,' said Cross, 'that is true. He has become ensnared by the Dark Mind. We have attempted to awaken him, but to no avail. Prendergast is a sleeping god. The flesh and all the trappings of this world keep him bound and in ignorance. It's a dream that has become too real.'

I still couldn't buy it. Obviously my facial expression said as much.

'You *still* don't believe?' wondered Cross.

I had already dismissed the forgotten novel and the date of bilocation. My twin could have been involved to create the illusion of this Prismatic Moderator having absolute knowledge. It could have been fed the information. The problem was Sandra and Joe in The Sandpiper. I couldn't have known about that, or arranged it to be so perfect a coincidence. Or the fact that Dave was the W-Day twin of David Cross. And that revelation was courtesy of Ding Dong, who knew nothing of the case.

'Cross,' I said, 'I need some air.'

'Fine,' he sighed, and stepped aside, nervously working the handle of the gun with a sweaty palm.

I stood up and turned to my twin, still holding his bloodied nose. 'Coming?'

I waved me away. 'I'll be fine.'

On the surface I saw Rochelle, seated on a block of stone, meditating. I said nothing so as not to disturb her.

Time to pull it all together, I thought. The answers had been less than forthcoming. Less than true, I felt. Something stank to high heaven. What was it? And what the Christ was that thing down there? Was it really part of the universe: an intelligent information processor working on a cosmic scale? Was it an alien?

I really needed a drink.

I walked over to the gate. It was locked, so I climbed over.

'Tommy, wait!' I heard Rochelle shouting in a panic. 'Shit, Tommy get back here!'

I was away.

After a few drinks I caught the bus back towards Hollywood. I decided that the office was not a safe place to be. I'd go crash at Ding Dong's for a while.

No, maybe not.

I knew a guy who owned a bar called 'Hot Knights' – a medieval-themed strip club – close to the studios. All the stars and film producers hung out there, getting their cocks rubbed by cheap ass. I needed space. Some time to think and drink and be alone. And you're never more alone than with a crowd of perverts getting a paid face full of pussy and talking business.

Chapter 29

Hot Knights was a sweat pit of flesh, loud music, poor ventilation and some of the biggest names in the business. If it wasn't for the fact that I knew Costas, the owner, I wouldn't have made it within spitting distance of the door.

Costas was one of the biggest, hardest bastards I ever met. I was glad to be a friend.

'Good to see you, Tommy,' he told me with a friendly embrace. 'We got some nice girls in tonight. I can introduce you if you want?'

'Actually Costas, I'm here to beg a favor.'

'Name it,' he said, putting an arm about my shoulders and leading me through the bar.

'I just need to spend a few days here, if that's okay. I'm working this case and...' I struggled to find the words.

Costas jumped in, saying, 'Don't worry about it, Tommy. You can stay as long as you want. As long as there's no trouble here, you understand?'

'No worries.'

'That's okay then. Let's get you a drink.'

I was sandwiched between Tina and Alexis. They were my companions for the night. Costas had sent them over to be real nice to me. We were talking about this and that and I was getting drunk. It was odd, because these two women wore medieval design bikinis and thongs. One even had a weapon that doubled – she told me – as a sex aid.

'It has this button,' she said, showing me, 'that starts this little motor and the ball and chain goes whizzing around! The spiky ball is like, plastic, or something. Really light, but the vibrations in the handle, baby! You wouldn't believe!' She leaned close to whisper in my ear. 'So when I get horny, I turn it on and gently push it up my cunt. The spiky ball goes round and round on that little chain and it just bashes against my thighs. I explode like a bomb! They should market this thing, you know?'

I had visions of the damn thing sticking out of her snatch, going round and round and taking off, her being hoisted into the air and floating out the window, floating above L.A. moaning and screaming.

I excused myself and made my way through the club, past the girls, the studio execs, the film stars and eventually over to the bar. I ordered a double scotch, no ice, and sat down on the bar stool. My body ached with tiredness. My mind felt revulsion towards all things. Everything had been soured by the Prismatic Moderator, by Cross, Rochelle and the whole fucking case.

Reality was now a thing of the past. It all seemed like a big joke. I could see how people would latch onto a concept such as the Dark Mind in times like this, but chances were – at least to my mind – that it was just another meaningless concept, and that the Dark Mind didn't actually exist. I drank the scotch and ordered another.

The more I thought about this case, the less I needed it, or the money. I was going to inform Prendergast that I had found his daughter, the whereabouts of Cross and let him deal with the rest. I wanted out of this shit. It was the same old typical insanity that this fucking place thrived on. It bred madness. It attracted the madmen and their prophets, and all the other religious crazies.

The night ended with that dildo-loving bitch riding my cock, rocking back and forth, her eyes closed, loving the fuck. She grunted like an animal every time I thrust. Jesus, Tina was a dirty little bitch and I loved every sweaty second of it. Between her breasts a small silver cross swayed back and forth upon a delicate chain. There was something erotic and blasphemous about the image of her sweaty tits and that crucifix.

Afterwards, we kissed and felt about as my dick stirred back into life. My attention was on her tits when I thought about the cross. I took the silver icon in my hand looked at it.

'It belonged to my mother' said Tina. 'It's beautiful, isn't it?'

There on the silver tree was the figure of Christ crucified – the Logos, nailed to a cross.

I remembered what the Prismatic Moderator had said. It all made sense. To set the Logos free, they were going to kill Prendergast.

Chapter 30

That's what all that religious, mystical crap meant. "Set free" and "release" were just sugar-coated words for *murder*. If Prendergast was a god, or Yahweh, or the Logos, or whatever, then in order to escape the material world and become this divine being once more, he had to *die*.

I left Tina asleep and slipped out of her apartment. I caught a cab back to the office. It was half three in the morning. Nobody was around. I paid the driver and stepped out into the cool night air.

Back in the office I turned on the light and, to my horror, found a huge scrawl of graffiti on the wall behind my trashed desk. It read:

DEAD MAN

'Shit!' I yelled, kicking the desk. I'd forgotten all about Jake's money. He was coming over personally to collect and I'd not been there. Christ, it really was the end. Pliers and Nose Ring were going to work my balls to mincemeat. There would be no possible way out of this one. I was fucked.

I slept on the couch in the office. I awoke at eight in the morning. I got up, made coffee, sat at the desk and made my plans. If I stayed in Hollywood, I was screwed. So, the first thing to do was to get out of Hollywood *alive*. That, itself, would be a miracle. I grabbed the phone and called a cab. The taxi would be there in a half hour. Once in the taxi, I would head back towards the coast, go back to Cross and try and halt this crazy motherfucker of a plan and maybe get a few more answers.

I picked up the phone and called Prendergast. There was no answer. Fuck it. I'd swing by in the taxi on my way back to the coast. If need be I'd put a goddamn note through his door. The phone rang. I picked up. It was Jake.

'Storm,' said Jake. 'You got my message?'

'Yeah, I got it. I suppose the Boys are on their way?'

'They soon will be.'

I sighed and figured it was worth a shot. 'Look, Jake, I fucked up. I'm sorry, but I'm here now, so why don't you come over for the money? Let's settle this like men. I was on a case, you know how it is.'

'I'm sorry, Tommy,' said Jake, 'but as soon as I hang up, I'm calling the Boys to sort this shit out. You brought this on yourself. Goodbye.'

And he was gone.

I sat there for a few moments, wondering what to do. The taxi would be here in ten minutes, but knowing Jake, the Boys were probably real close so as to nail my ass before I could escape. But I've been wrong before.

I leapt out from behind the desk and grabbed my trilby. On the way down the stairs I remembered my old, faithful Berkeley was still back at The Sandpiper Hotel.

Chapter 31

I made it out of the building and ran, but a car – the car – was already pulling up and out got Pliers.

'Time's up, baby!' he bellowed, pointing a finger at me, 'your lily-white balls are mine, motherfucker!'

I heard myself say 'Aw, fuck!' and then I ran. I didn't stop running. I knew he was behind me. I knew Nose Ring was following in the car, ready to make a move. *Just keep moving*, I told myself, *if you stop, you die.*

I pushed my way past and through people, heading towards god alone knows. I ran past the tacky souvenir stores, past the multiplexes, past the gawping, gawking faces of everybody who could have helped me, the sound of Shrapnel gaining with every curse from his lips.

I decided to make a break across the Hollywood boulevard. Maybe get lucky and be hit by a car. Anything was better than having my balls split and ripped open by pliers. I timed it badly. Nose Ring clipped me as I raced across a junction. I heard horns sounding as I hit the concrete. Somebody got a hold of me and pulled me to my feet.

'You should have saved your strength,' hissed Pliers, dragging me to the car, 'you'll need it.'

I kicked and yelled, lashing out, hoping and praying that somebody would make a stand, but this was L.A. and self-preservation was the Golden Rule in this town, this city of the no good and fallen.

In the car, Pliers punched me twice in the face to knock the fight out of me. I heard him say to Nose Ring, 'Turn it up', and the music got real loud. Pliers quickly took off my trousers and pulled down my shorts. My cock and balls were for the taking. I felt the pliers against my skin, a burning pain, I reacted quickly bringing up my knee and smashing the son-of-a-bitch in the nose. I heard the bone crack. Blood sprayed the window. Nose Ring was trying to pull over but I grabbed the pliers and jammed them into his shoulder. He screamed. The car was out of control. We were hit by another vehicle and over we went.

Chapter 32

I crawled out of the car holding my bleeding balls in one hand and my trousers in the other. I examined the damage. One of my nuts had been cut, but not too badly. It looked worse than it actually was, but it sure as hell didn't feel that way. I pulled on my trousers. A small crowd was gathering. A siren could be heard. I made tracks, checking over my shoulder to see Pliers limping away, holding his face. Nose Ring was still in the car.

The sight of a man limping through the streets of L.A. holding his balls in blood-stained trousers, his left hand in tatters, his face cut and bruised went – as I knew it would – completely unnoticed. I had just fled the scene of an accident, my finger-prints were sure as hell on the pliers sticking out of Nose Ring's shoulder and the cops would soon be all over my ass like an inmate gangbang in the prison showers. That, too, was more than likely unless I could settle this shit and clear my name.

The first thing I did was to get a rental car. Fuck the taxi. I'd drive over to Prendergast and warn him, then head on back to the Prismatic Moderator for some answers and hopefully win the girl (or at the very least fuck her) and nail Cross to his namesake. I'd be a hero. I didn't know to whom exactly and I'm pretty sure my plan was so full of holes it could have been dreamed up by any number of asshole wannabe writers at Ding Dong's, but I truly didn't give a fuck. You tend not to when some crazy prick has just tried ripping your balls off.

I was back on the case.

Chapter 33

I was close to the Prendergast homestead. I was thinking so hard my brain hurt. Pulling all the pieces together to try and understand all this madness. Why would Rochelle want to kill her own father? What was with the trick in the hotel room? Who was she really? Well, if Prendergast was a god, and she was the daughter, then I could only assume she'd picked up some of daddy's divine abilities. And how did Cross get to be involved in all this? From what I could see, he was too weak and cowardly, like most industry types, to actually be capable of anything other than stand in front of a camera, look pretty, and say words that had been put into his mouth by some brainless hack. My hunch about Cross was that life simply imitated art. No, it was the lovely Rochelle behind this, I was certain. The delectable mystic two-faced bitch!

I parked the car outside the house. The gate was shut. I tried the intercom but no answer, so I made my way around the side of the house to find another way in. It was high walls all the way round. I waited for a time but there was no sign of life. I made a decision; if I was going to save his useless fat backside I was going to have to haul my bleeding nuts back to face Rochelle and the Prismatic Moderator in double quick time. I got back into the car and drove. Time was on the march.

Back at The Sandpiper I staggered past reception and up the stairs to my room. Once there I discovered that I had lost the key. I rested my head against the door, banging some sense into it, and then just kicked the bastard open. Problem solved.

Inside I showered and then cleaned and bandaged what I could, returning to the bedroom to be greeted by the glorious sight of my old gumshoe suit and Berkeley. I smiled.

That evening I drove back to the building site. I was tired, and from memory it took me some time to find it, but I was back on the case, remember?

I parked up some way from the gates and waited for darkness before I made my move. I climbed the fence and dropped into the site, ready for a showdown. I was going to kick some serious ass, get some answers, save Prendergast from these religious nuts and hopefully get the girl. I didn't care which girl, but I figured I deserved one after the day I had.

I saw movement. Voices could be heard. I ducked behind some junk and peered over the rim of broken concrete and stripped electrical cable. I saw me. I saw me with Rochelle. They were talking, walking slowly, and it looked as if she was explaining something to me and I was hanging off every word.

I figured I could make it past them and head down into the basement to confront Cross. I'd make him confess to their plans. He was the weakest of the three. He'd crack, the poor sap.

I was about to make a move when I saw something amazing. Rochelle was slowly lifting her cotton dress to reveal her body. Off it came and every luscious curve glowed with an alluring radiance in the moonlight. Then I saw her kiss me. I returned the kiss, nice and slow, allowing my lucky hands to explore her breasts and ass. I even slipped a finger or two up the holy of holies. I was furious! The bitch loved it. She let her head hang back as I kissed her neck, and then took her against the wall, hurriedly unzipping to release my cock. She wrapped her legs about me and I slowly pushed in my length. We fucked, passion-ately, free of inhibitions, there right in front of me. It was a coupling I could only ever dream about and a strange sadness weighed upon my heart. The way she looked at *him*, but not at me. The fact that she would give herself to the twin, but I was something that needed to be trained like an animal. I moved on, cursing my luck.

I found Cross asleep on the floor outside the room housing the Prismatic Moderator. I stepped over him and into the room. This time I stood before the Prismatic Moderator, and I tried to gaze upon it face on. It was like a tunnel of fire and light raging in eternity. I tried but it was still all too much.

'Twin,' it said, every word engulfing me like a blast of power, 'what do you wish to know?'

'Who are you? What are you really?' I shouted over the sound of fury.

'I am,' began the Moderator, 'what I am.'

'Are you also a god?'

'God is a human concept, Twin. This all plays out in the lower realm of truth. You can call me a god if you wish.'

'No,' I shot back, 'I don't believe in god!'

'Neither do I,' said the Moderator.

This surprised me. 'Is there anything?'

'Oh, there's plenty,' replied the Moderator in a matter of fact tone, 'but utterly beyond human comprehension. There are limitless truths, Twin. Things I could speak of, but you have no words for. It would be as a man talking to an amoeba or politician. Rather one-sided.'

'You told me Prendergast was a god.'

'I used words and terminology that you could understand.'

'What about Rochelle,' I asked, 'what is she?'

'She is the daughter of Anthony Prendergast.'

This didn't help.

The Moderator continued, saying, 'Again, using familiar concepts – she is divine, like Prendergast – she is a child of a god. What you experienced in the hotel room was her attempts to push you out of the Dark Mind and into her realm of thought and of experience. In the end, you attained that state, for a time.'

I thought about what the Moderator was saying. 'So, all that sex stuff, the flirtation, the teasing was her way of...' I lost the thread of my reason. God, this was confusing.

'She was leading you through the prison of your own desires, Twin. You refused her at the end. Feed a child enough chocolate and it will become sick of its own cravings. That was the breakthrough, for what it was worth. And in my examining of the information, it was worth very little for it was short-lived.'

I could have asked so much more, but you know what it's like. In hindsight you should have said this or that. I never did ask how Cross got be involved in this mess. Later I could only assume the answer. Nor did I discover how Rochelle had learnt of her true identity, or of that of her father. Nor did I ask how Edward Scissorhands miraculously found all that ice in that stupid Tim Burton movie. Was it delivered and how did he sign for it? Again, I could only assume. The one thing foremost in my mind, dark or otherwise, was my involvement in this cosmic caper.

The Prismatic Moderator spoke again.

'Throughout your history, the demiurge has immersed his divine self into the creation he so jealously guards. His love is smothering and controlling, for he wants nothing but your attention and praise and worship. He knows no different, for he is an ignorant child. And when mankind's worship is shifted to another focus, he steps in to become that new object of devotion. In this way he can be worshipped, control it and be satiated.'

'Hollywood,' I said with a nod. 'Good Christ, why am I *not* surprised?'

'Mankind's energy and focus of worship is fame. For the demiurge, it is the golden calf he will steal away. He will do this by becoming a vital part of what is the form of new worship.'

I wasn't impressed. 'Yeah, that's great. Instead of following a God, we create film stars and musicians as our heroes. They get to save the world for us, highlighting issues and telling us to hand over our money to make a difference. Then they go home to their fucking multi-million dollar lifestyles as poor Joe Blow on minimum wage is suckered into helping the starving children of the world, barely able to support himself. What an improvement!'

'Your choice,' said the Moderator, flatly.

A sudden blow of information punched into my head from the Prismatic Moderator. It was a mind-bending catalogue of such painful atrocity, cruelty and social injustice that I shook my head violently, trying to spill the images out of my mind's eye so as to make it all unseen.

'This is the legacy,' the prismatic Moderator continued, 'and this is what happens when the information does not flow. If life does not thrive, it turns against itself and destroys, becoming useless and stagnant. Stagnation is the true destroyer. The prison of the Dark Mind is simply the construct wherein such destruction takes place.'

The images stopped and I groaned with relief.

'That is not the worst I could have shown you, Twin.'

I was tired, feeling broken and defeated by this case. It was impossible to grasp such madness. I decided to call it quits. I was going to leave these crazy assholes to plan their crime, go back to the hotel, get shit-faced and head home in the morning.

I wondered where I was. Was I still with Rochelle, screwing her brains out, or what? I asked the Prismatic Moderator.

'You are driving towards Beverley Hills,' it replied.

It took a few moments to register, but then I realized.

I was going to kill Prendergast.

Chapter 34

I left the room, tripping over the still sleeping Cross, cursing loudly, but the guy just snorted and snored and whined like a puppy. I noticed a bottle of vodka on the table. It was empty. Cross was shitfaced and out for the count. I kicked him. Hell, I kicked him hard in the head, hoping to knock some goddamn sense into his addled brain cells. I detested the overpaid fuck. Worshipped by millions, I could understand why Prendergast – if he were a god – wanted to control his every move and to be the one responsible for his grand success: the big man behind the scenes. A huge cock up Cross's ass, giving him the slow pleasurable fuck of fame.

I made my way out of the basement, up into the cool night air. The sky was a thick tangle of stars. What a fucking mess. No wonder the world was fucked. Everything was chaos and insanity. Prendergast had let us all down. Yeah, maybe he was god – a god, *the* God – I didn't know. Nothing made sense and that was all I had to go on!

Okay, I was going to have to work on the presumption that all of this bullshit was true. It seemed the only way to get through this nightmare and save myself. Yeah, that's right, I. Fuck Prendergast, fuck the god-slayers, fuck the box office receipts of *The Dark Mind* and fuck the prison of the Dark Mind to boot! This was a simple case of self-preservation now.

As I blundered up the steps and out into the eerie quiet of the building site, Rochelle Prendergast was waiting for me, gun in hand.

'Please,' she said, 'don't make me kill you. There is no afterlife for the likes of you. Not yet. You've not evolved it yet.'

'The likes of *me*,' I spat back. 'And I guess the Pope waltzes into Paradise with a hard-on!'

She smiled. 'Mankind has not yet evolved the ability to

survive physical death. Not yet, anyway. My father doesn't want you too. It keeps you in your place, see?'

Now I was only joking, being a smart ass, see? She was being serious. Her tone of voice convinced me. And if these were the gods, I didn't want to piss them off and go straight to the blank just yet.

'You have to believe me, Storm,' Rochelle began, walking forward, gun level at my gut, 'this is the only way for mankind to be freed from the Dark Mind. It's the only way mankind can be liberated by the Savior and shown the one true path.'

'What Savior?'

Rochelle placed a hand upon her belly. 'The Savior is the one who will open the eyes of mankind to the ways of my father. He will liberate mankind, and my father will finally be usurped. Mankind will finally be able to evolve spiritually, to realize and follow the ways of the Savior. The future is written in good deeds and we all will follow a godly path.'

'What about our own path?' I said. 'Do we not have a say in any of this? You all seem to know what's best for us. How about allowing us to make up our own minds for a change?'

She laughed. 'You are not ready for such responsibility! You need to be taught such things.'

'Oh? And who made you such an expert on what's right or wrong for mankind? You're about to commit murder!'

'It's not murder!'

'You're taking a man's life!'

'He is not a man!'

I thought fast. 'All you're doing is replacing one prison with another. You're thinking for us! How is that freedom?'

These words struck a nerve. I saw her flinch. 'That's not true.'

I took a step forward. 'Rochelle, please, killing your father is not the answer. There has to be another way!'

'No,' she said, raising the gun higher. It was now level with my face. I almost pissed myself. I squirmed under the gaze of the barrel. 'This has always been the way,' she continued. 'There has never been another way. It is simply how it's done. There has always been a chosen one to perform the act.'

'Who was the last?'

'Judas Iscariot,' she said. 'He was the last big name. A few others have emerged but in his last incarnation, the Logos was killed by accident. He was killed in a train wreck in Germany during World War Two.'

'Wait a second,' I said, thinking back to Judas, '*Jesus* was the jealous God?'

Rochelle shook her head. 'No. It was the temple guard, Saul. After Jesus was put to death, Saul became Paul and the rest is dogma. He stole the light of the Messiah and turned his message into another prison.'

'The crafty fucker,' I mused.

'That's why Judas repented and killed himself. He was given the wrong information. He got the wrong man.'

I nodded. 'I'm cold and I need a piss.'

Rochelle indicated with the gun to her right. There was a concrete wall. 'Use it,' she said. 'You're not going anywhere, Tommy Storm. Not until it's over.'

'Fuck,' I grumbled taking my place at the wall. How the hell was I going to get away and save the day? And how was I ever going to force a piss with a woman behind me holding a gun?

Chapter 35

Eventually it came.

'Thank God,' said Rochelle. 'I thought you might have been jerking off, or something.'

'You want to shake the drips off?'

Rochelle grimaced. 'Oh, please.'

I zipped up and turned around. 'You didn't seem to have a problem handling it before, as I remember.'

She was quick to blush. 'Mind your own business, Storm.'

'We can always pass the time the same way?'

'In your dreams!' she snapped.

'Aw, come on! I mean, what's the difference?'

'The difference is that I love him. I love him because he's everything you're not. He was making the break from the Dark Mind long before I met him.'

'Ah, of course he was. I forgot. He's a saint.'

'He's the father of the Savior,' she said.

I was stunned.

'That's right,' she confirmed, tightening her grip on the gun.

Now I was pissed. 'So how the hell did you do it, huh?'

'Do what?'

'Brainwash me!'

'I didn't. You – I mean, he – just saw and he believed. He just knew in his heart the truth. It can happen. It's called pure faith.'

'Pure shit!'

The gun jerked towards me. 'Watch it, Storm! I'll kill you if I have to!'

Behind the cowering, I mustered up some courage. 'Ah, thank God you're here to show us the way, Rochelle! What would we do without you and your bastard Savior? What a better world it will be as you control and brainwash and lead the way forward to a glorious future of disguised servitude and divine ass kissing! Oh,

and FUCK YOU WHORE!'
    Unsurprisingly, she fired the gun.

PART TWO

Chapter 36

A year later and I was limping my sorry out-of-work ass to the bar for a drink. It was a hot day. My hip was playing up again. I was convinced I had bone cancer. It truly felt as if a curse had been put upon where that bitch Rochelle Prendergast shot me. The doctors dug around and removed the bullet, leaving me with a severe limp and practically constant pain. All I could take was pain killers, which I did, but knocked back with enough goddamn drink to ensure they worked. I might've been out of my fucking tree half the time, but at least I wasn't in pain.

I entered The Majestic – and as shitty as bars got, The Majestic was the tops.

'Conrad,' said Alvin, the fat and friendly barkeep. 'What can I get you?'

'A beer, thanks,' I replied. I winced as I sat down on the barstool.

'That damned leg again, huh?'

'Yeah,' I grunted, reaching for the painkillers in my jacket pocket. 'It's a son-of-a-bitch today and no doubt.'

'Here, Conrad,' said Alvin, placing the cool beer on the bar before me, 'it's on the house.'

Alvin might have run the shittiest bar I'd ever frequented, but he was a true gent. I told him so.

I toasted Alvin and The Majestic, but lost my spirit upon drinking. I needed to escape. After all, I was no longer Tommy Storm. Tommy Storm was dead. Now I was Conrad Stone. I'd called in a few favors to change my identity. I had to stay low. Now the police wouldn't be looking for me for stabbing Nose Ring and, if they were convinced that Tommy Storm was no more, I guessed Jake and Pliers would be off my case too.

As for Prendergast, Cross and the Prismatic Moderator, I couldn't be so sure. If the Moderator knew everything and was still in cahoots with Rochelle and Cross, then they would be able to find me. I was going on the hypothesis that information flowed to the Moderator via consciousness, so my plan was to just stay as shitfaced as possible and give him the slip. I was unemployed, collecting benefit and drinking all the way to the last full stop.

And if consciousness was not the key and the Prismatic Moderator still saw me, well then at least it would know that I was not a threat. What could a man in my condition do? I considered all of this as I drank. And every damn time somebody walked into the bar I panicked, thinking that they'd found me.

Later that night I hobbled my ass past Ding Dong's. The bar was busy. Full of life and sound and I could even see the kid tending bar. No sign of Ding Dong, though. I'd not seen her for a year. No doubt she'd heard of my death. Christ, she'd be over me by now. A bum like me meant nothing to a woman like that. She was probably up stairs riding another white cock, telling some chump that he had the biggest dick she'd ever had the sweet privilege to fuck. Yeah, I was ashes by now for sure. All dust and forgotten. It began to rain. I headed home.

"Home" was an apartment in downtown L.A. on the third floor above a sleazy wedding chapel run by Latinos. Some days I helped out by filming the weddings on a small digital camera. They paid me five bucks a shoot. It was beer money, so I didn't complain. And the amount of weddings these guys could fit in a day meant I could walk away with a good forty dollars if I stuck it out. Most days I didn't. I did an hour or two then walked. I couldn't stand them to be honest. The weddings that is; Latinos are fine by me.

Chapter 37

It was a Saturday. I was in bed. My hip felt as if it was being gnawed down to the bone. I was sweating. Probably dying, I thought, because I'd popped an awful lot of pills during the night and all washed down with vodka. Maybe I was fucked, but I didn't care. At least death would be the end of it, if Rochelle Prendergast were to be believed.

Was it true? Was any of it true? The thought still reeled in my mind. The moment I started to believe I got messy and took a bullet. I let delusion cloud my view. I started talking to the gods instead of people, arguing the toss and bargaining for a better world instead of saving my own ass. What an asshole. What a fucking mistake.

I couldn't stand the pain anymore. I got out of bed. It was little more than a stained linen sop of my sweat. It stank of body odor and alcohol, like some grotesque dead man's shroud. 'It's what future generations will remember me by' I said to myself, opening the window to let in some air.

I looked out but did not see. All I could think of was the child. How old now: three, maybe four months? What would Tommy Storm make of it all? Ah, but Tommy was dead and saw nothing. He remembered nothing, not even the lovely Rochelle, his child, the mission to slay a god and free the world from the Dark Mind – or making a fatal detour that night.

I ran over the events again.

After leaving Rochelle, Tommy drove back towards Beverley Hills to kill Prendergast, but for whatever reason, he drove back into Hollywood to the office. Having no idea that I was a marked man, he was taken out – I could only presume – by Pliers, who was waiting to finish the job and bust my ass for the crash and sticking it to Nose Ring. Tommy Storm never made it to the Prendergast house.

All I could remember was blacking out, Rochelle Prendergast standing over me. I've no idea what happened to them – to Cross or Rochelle after that. I awoke in the hospital, registered as a John Doe, no ID or medical records to go on. I kept quiet. Told them my name was Conrad and that I'd been mugged and, no, I didn't want to press charges. Conrad was an old drinking buddy from way back. He was probably dead by now. Last I heard he'd skipped the pond back home, probably drank himself to death. That was a good ten years ago. Nobody cared to check my story. Nobody cared, full stop. Like I said, welcome to L.A.

I wondered again how Tommy's kid was doing. The Savior of the world, you know? The lucky little bastard was probably sucking on Rochelle's tit right now.

Chapter 38

The movie *The Dark Mind* was a global box office hit. It became the third-highest grossing movie of all time. Its heady mix of action, sex and David Cross ensured that Prendergast became the biggest producer working in Hollywood. He was already hard at work on a sequel called *The Virus Inside*. He promised, and I quote:

> *'The Virus Inside' takes the character of Jensen Bow (David Cross) to an even deeper level of intrigue than 'The Dark Mind'. We had to compromise on that film. A lot was cut to accommodate a reasonable running time, but was re-instated in the extended home retail release. In the sequel we just run with it! People want to go with us on this journey!'*

He continues:

> *'The idea that mankind is facing a great struggle against seemingly invincible forces strikes a chord in us all. We all face these struggles each and every day. It's up to us to make a difference and I believe that is the primary duty of film and of all art in general. It's to say what needs to be said in such a way that it reaches a large audience. I believe that as artists, we have that responsibility.'*

Jesus Christ! Would somebody *please* shoot this asshole? Tommy Storm, where are you when we need you?

I dropped the magazine onto the table and sighed. There was Anthony Prendergast, staring right back at me from behind his glossy, full color sheen. I placed my hot coffee mug over his tanned, fat face. It left a damp ring. It could just as easily have been the residue from his own dick he'd been gloriously sucking on all through the article, the pompous fat-looking fuck.

I scratched my beard. It was itchy and ached to be shaved clean off, but I couldn't do that. I'd also let my hair grow long. I couldn't even wear the Berkeley. I just couldn't risk it. I was convinced they were looking for me. I had to stay hidden.

After coffee I made my way to the cemetery. It was situated next to the studios, which was either ironic or a fact of life in the industry. And by that I mean many once famous people are buried there. And so was I.

Rochelle Prendergast, in the throes of grief, had erected a monument to Tommy Storm down by the lake. A monstrous tomb adorned with angels and the saints. Sweet Christ, it looked so ridiculously kitsch and camp, Liberace would have thought twice about it. A fine monument indeed to a hard-ass, hard drinking son-of-a-bitch like me – except Tommy Storm was none of those things. Not the Storm that actually worked, anyway. He was a clean-cut prick, for sure. I was the bum – the lousy drunk with a hard-on for pussy and bullshit.

It was hot that day. My shirt was soaked wet and clinging to my weary frame. I was wearing a short-cut leather jacket and could smell my own stink. I sat down on the grass by the lake, reached into the jacket and pulled out a hipflask. I took a hit or two.

My mind was brimming with misery. I took a strange comfort from the presence of the dead. Once famous, now fucked, just like me. What the hell was any of it for? Knowing there was a God (of sorts) was of no comfort, for he was delusional in heaven and on earth. And if Rochelle was right, then everybody slept in darkness once dead. As if they had never existed in the first place. What a deal.

I felt the scar twinge and let rip a fierce burn. I winced and took another hit of the bottle. Goddamn it! What a fucking misery. Next stop: extinction. As I took a swig I froze. There was movement. Somebody had ducked behind a monument across the lake. They'd lost sight of me and accidentally wandered into my field of vision. I'd done it myself a good few times. Hell, I'd blown many an assignment that way, but I guess my excuse was that I was probably drunk at the time.

In short: I was being followed.

Chapter 39

They'd found me – there was no other possible answer.

I was hammering home a beer at a nasty gay bar called 'Heave-Ho', convinced that the Prismatic Moderator had honed in on my thoughts – on the information supplied by my own actions – and finally tracked me down. Chances are that information had been passed onto Rochelle, and the snoop in the cemetery was a miserable no good son-of-a-bitch gumshoe, just like myself. Only, *that* miserable gumshoe lowlife chicken-fucker was actually employed.

'Hey, need company?' said a short guy next to me at the bar. He was wearing a tight-fitting vest and jeans. His hair was short and the copious gold earrings caught what little light the Heave-Ho had to offer.

'No, thanks,' I said and returned to my drink.

'C'mon!' teased the guy, 'Let me buy you a drink! You look as if you need filling up!' And he laughed at his own innuendo as if it was actually funny.

'No, really,' I said, 'besides, I'm not queer.'

'That's what they all say!'

'No, really, I just wanted a drink.'

Now at this his attitude changed somewhat. He became brusque and confrontational. 'What are you doing here, then?' he demanded.

I showed him my glass. 'I needed a drink.'

'Yeah, I know why you are here, but this isn't a place for people like you.'

'People like me?' It took me a few moments to figure this out. 'You mean straight people?'

'Well, yeah.'

I placed my glass on the bar and faced him. I towered a good few inches above him but he had the muscles. I had to be careful.

I had a point to make but didn't want to fight this homo. I was simply too drunk. He'd beat the shit out of me and I knew it. I think he knew it too.

I began by saying, 'You know that's like me saying a guy like you can't drink in a regular bar, but you do, don't you? I mean, you don't just drink in gay bars, right?'

No answer. Was he going to hit me?

I continued. 'So, denying me the right to drink in a gay bar is like the exact opposite of homophobia: *heterophobia*! And in these enlightened times I expected a little more from a guy like you, frankly. That's segregation, man! Burn a fucking cross outside my house, why don't you? I'm very disappointed in you.'

Now the short guy looked at me for a few seconds and then he said, 'Take it easy, I'm sorry. Enjoy your drink.'

As he walked away, I didn't feel a sense of victory because I didn't believe a fucking word I'd just said. Such noble sentiments failed to spark within my breast. I just wanted to drink and not get hassled.

A little time later the same short guy – now drunk – came up to me and put his meaty arm about my shoulders, slurring into my ear 'If you were gay, I'd fuck you in a heartbeat.'

'I'll take that as a compliment,' I said, slipping from his grip and leaving the bar.

It was raining outside. I pulled the tatty coat about me, shivering. I felt sick, like I was coming down with the flu. My whole body ached. My throat was raw and my mouth dry. I could barely spit. I needed another drink.

I caught the subway back home. It was late. I sat next to a fat kid in jeans and a T-shirt reading a film magazine. He was a student, I guessed.

'Man,' he said to me, 'you like movies?'

'Not really.'

'Man, how can you not like movies? This is the movie capital of the world! This is L.A.! Jesus Christ!'

I was wrong. He was just another fucking tourist.

'Have you seen that film *The Dark Mind*? Man, that's awesome. Have you seen it? Man, now *that's* a movie. You don't like movies? Check it out. It will *totally* convert you, man. You'll love it. *Everybody* loves that film!'

I turned to the kid. 'That's the one with David Cross, right?'

'Yeah, that's right! Man, he's at the top of his game right now.'

'Yeah, he's also a queer.'

'He's a what?'

'A fudge-packer, a trouser bandit, a lover of the one-eyed serpent of Eden, you know what I mean?'

'Man, that's bullshit! He's married! He's got kids!'

'It's a front,' I shot back. 'He's a queer. He pretends to be straight so as to appeal to a wider audience. Middle America. The God-fearing Christian types, you know? It's all about money. The studios want every fucking dollar they can squeeze out of you gullible pricks, reading your fan magazines and never wondering why any movie that places advertising space within its pages never gets a bad notice. Money, friend, is what movies are all about.'

'Jesus, that's so cynical! I want to be a director, man, and films are more than just about money! The director has a vision to put across! It's art, at the end of the day.'

'No, it isn't. It's *commerce*. That's what you tourists don't understand. Hollywood doesn't want artists, kid. It just wants money.'

I made it back to the apartment and spewed up.

Later, I cooked myself a few eggs and forced them down along with some sweet English tea. I felt better. I made another cup, drank that, and felt better still. But I still wanted to drink. The desire, ache, need, craving, drive – whatever you want to call it – was like a beast squirming in my stomach, parched and dry, desperate for liquor in order to be quenched. Christ, I was thirsty for a drink. I needed a drink. And I wanted to keep on drinking.

I had to have a drink!

I searched the apartment and found a mini bottle of tequila. A gift I had never opened because I hate the stuff. I opened it anyway and poured myself a shot. Down it went. It tasted foul. I poured another and another and down they went. Each hit as lousy as the last. Pretty soon the bottle was gone. I was still thirsty. That dry, cracking beast was barely moist and my stomach was raw. I looked again and found another mini bottle of tequila under the bed. Half full, soon empty. I went to the toilet and puked the whole lot up. There was blood in the mix of eggs, tea and liquor.

A few days passed. I stayed inside, chewed up by a fever. I drank water. No booze, except a nip here and there when the shakes kicked in. I hallucinated that the family Prendergast were in the room, talking loudly about movies. The Child Messiah was bouncing on my bed and shouting 'Bouncy, bouncy!' over and over and laughing. Tommy was there, looking fondly at the child and Rochelle, but he slinked away without a word.

And then after the fever broke, I slept solidly for sixteen hours. I did not even dream. I was as good as dead.

When I awoke it was dark. I checked my watch. It was about eleven. I fancied a drink, so crawled out of bed to the kitchen and poured myself a shot of whisky.

Yeah, it tasted good. It tasted too good. I distinctly remember not having any whisky the other night, only tequila. And I knew that if I turned around I was bound to see the gumshoe from the cemetery stood behind the kitchen door, glass in one hand, loaded pistol in the other.

'Don't sweat it,' he said, 'I never carry a gun.'

I turned. 'Who sent you?'

The gumshoe stepped forward, smiling. 'Mr Prendergast would like a word.'

Chapter 40

Now the gumshoe was called Eddie. He was from the East coast, a New Yorker. His stock was Irish and a flame of red hair curled about his fat face. He wheezed a little and was out of shape. Then again, so was I. To make matters worse my clothes were now hanging on me. I'd lost so much weight with the fever, the drink and the whole shebang, the old suit looked at least two sizes too big.

I decided to shave the beard, slick back the long hair and resurrect Tommy – if only for this meeting. I needed him to face Prendergast and not take any shit. I had a vague feeling what this was all about. Once it was over, I would crawl back into the shell of Conrad and continue to drink him dead.

Eddie waited in the car as I humped my crippled ass up to the Prendergast house. I rang the bell and waited, pain dancing through my body.

'Hi, Tommy,' said Rochelle, opening the door.

I said nothing for a few moments. I just stared at her and she laughed and stepped back, opening the door wide.

'Come on in,' she said. 'Daddy's in the office. He'll be out in a minute.'

'Thanks,' I said, wondering why I wasn't strangling this insane bitch. Was this a set-up? Was this part of her plan?

'I'm just working on some material for the show, you want to see?'

I was dumbfounded. 'You have a show?'

'Yeah,' said Rochelle, leading me through the house by the arm. 'It's like a self-help show. People write in with their problems and I help them on my show. And every week I'm accompanied by a special guest. On the first show it was David Cross, the actor? Last week it was that guy who wrote that book about taking control of your life and getting what you really want. You know the guy I mean.'

'I don't read.'

'You should read his book, Tommy. It might help you, you know? It's helped so many people.'

'Mr Storm?' said Prendergast, his voice booming down the corridor. 'This way, please.' I hobbled towards Prendergast.

Chapter 41

Prendergast sat me down in his office. He didn't sit. He paced about the room in circles. He did laps around me, so he drifted in and out of my vision and dwindled around the back.

'I asked you here to talk about the money you owe me.'

'That I owe you?'

'Yes, the sum of money that I paid you in advance to find my daughter.'

'She's here, isn't she?'

'Indeed she is, thank God, but with very little contribution from you, Thomas. And considering that the individual I actually hired was tragically killed, I feel that the money you kept should be returned. I didn't give the money to you, per se, but to your other self.'

'The other Tommy Storm,' I finished, wearily.

'I hired your business partner to find out about my daughter, and instead he exploited her. He abused my trust. And trust is not something I give easily. I asked you to find my daughter and you also abused that trust. You failed in your job and you kept the money for it.'

'Hey! That money was *ours*. It belonged to the business. We were one and the same, Tommy and I, remember?'

'That's not true' said Prendergast. 'Would you consider David Cross's twin self to be as his original self?'

I thought of Dave. 'Okay, no, but...'

'Indeed not,' cut in Prendergast, standing behind me. 'Did you know that Cross is now in a similar position to yourself?'

I turned around to face Prendergast, but he moved again. 'Dave's dead?'

'Cross found him in his swimming pool three months ago. He had taken his own life.'

I wasn't shocked by this. Strangely, I felt deeply saddened.

'How did Cross react?'

'I really don't know. I can't say that I particularly care.' He sat on the desk opposite me. 'The investigation was a complete farce, Thomas. And I am politely asking for you to return my money. This will be the only time that I ask you. Do you understand?'

I felt like a child. 'Yes,' I muttered, caving in. What the fuck was wrong with me?

'If you fail to return my money in the time that we will now agree between us,' he gestured to somebody unseen behind me, 'then I will have to use other means.'

Pliers stood at my side.

'It's a small world,' said Prendergast, smiling.

'Yeah,' said Pliers. 'Isn't it just?'

Prendergast knew Jake it turned out. Upon finding out that I was still alive Jake offered Prendergast the loan of Plier's services.

Yeah. It's a small world.

Prendergast gave me a month to find the money. He told me that Pliers was hired to follow me twenty-four seven if need be. So, the chances of skipping town were slim.

Prendergast escorted me back through the house. I was fuming, but what could I do? I had lost. Trying to resurrect Tommy had failed. I just sat there taking it. I had no nerve. Tommy was dead. And a piece of me had died with him.

'Where's the baby?' I suddenly asked Prendergast.

'That's none of your concern,' he shot back, coldly. And then he slowed down, taking hold of my arm. 'Actually,' he began with a smile.

Chapter 42

Now he led me by the arm, as though we were old friends, through the house and up the stairs to the top floor. And there was the nursery. There was a name on the door: Kyle. It was painted in big funky looking letters. We stepped inside.

There was a carer sitting on a chair. She stood up when we entered. Prendergast excused her and allowed me to walk over to the cot. It took a moment to sink in.

There was the Child Messiah. He was both physically and mentally handicapped.

'My daughter's little rebellion ended here,' said Prendergast.

I turned to look at him and wondered just how much he actually knew. I wanted to ask him, to get a confession and the truth, but I didn't. I didn't see any point. I just moved quietly out of the room, away from the fat fucker and the handicapped Christ. I felt nothing for either of them.

Back in the car, Eddie lit up and dropped me back home. He whistled all the way.

I knew that if I needed any solid answers, the only one who could help me would be the Prismatic Moderator, but that would be up to it to approach me. Until then, I had to make do with guess work. And this was the best theory I could come up with.

I figured that after Tommy's death, Rochelle clung onto the child as the only hope she had to overthrow her father's dominion. I guess the kid also reminded her of Tommy, but Kyle being handicapped was something (in her mind at least) that was unacceptable. It destroyed her. It wasn't a fruition of her plans or justification for Tommy's death. So, in this fragile state of mind she returns to Daddy and the fat fuck takes over.

Now she's back in the bubble and he's controlling her success. And, thanks to *The Dark Mind*, his newfound status allows him to land her a show that enlists some of the biggest names in the industry. And how the hell Cross wormed his way off the hook is anybody's guess. Did Prendergast actually link him in with Rochelle at any point?

A few days later I made my way through the door of Ding Dong's. The bar was empty. I ordered a beer. There was a sign above the bar reading 'UNDER NEW MANAGEMENT: DON'T FUCK WITH ME.'

I abandoned my drink and left.

Chapter 43

A week later I received a letter. It was from Rochelle. Part of it said,

> *'I want to help people from now on.*
> *That's what they really need.'*

And then a quote from a book called 'The Dark Mind' by Edward Pendle. The book was published in 1901, she informed me, and she had recently discovered it.

Here's the quote in full:

> *'Is man, then, more compassionate than his God? This is the highest hope we can cling to. For if we can surrender Judgment, close the gates of Heaven and extinguish the fires of Hell, how brightly would we shine? How perfected would we be? And how pale in comparison our highest and most sublime models of Divinity when placed next to our own example!'*

Along with the letter was a check for the exact amount I owed Prendergast. My ass was saved!

I never saw Rochelle again but she did send me a letter from an undisclosed location. It was a good year on from the check and I was back in business as Tommy Storm. Now, this letter from Rochelle explained a great deal and in painful detail, but I won't quote verbatim if you don't mind. Life's too short. Needless to say she'd sought help to overcome her initial rejection of Kyle and to cope with the death of Tommy. I doubt the therapist helped her plot a god's demise, but I check the papers every day in the vain hope I'm wrong.

She had also quit the show and Hollywood (much to the disgust of Prendergast) and also left home, starting a new life with Kyle, holding down a regular job and training for a new career (undisclosed to the likes of me). She was blunt about everything that had happened. She apologized to me for certain things, but strangely *not* for shooting me – the lousy cunt. She also told me that the chance discovery of the book by Edward Pendle had been the first step towards recovery after her apparent breakdown. The passage she quoted me had changed her view on a lot of things. She now thought it possible to *'love my father out of power'*. I'm not sure what that meant, but any sleight against Prendergast was fine by me.

She concluded, saying:

'I'm sorry I let him control me at a weak moment. That divine seduction was an easy crutch and comfort at a bad time in my life. I'm trying to forgive him. You should do the same. Goodbye, Tommy Storm.'

And then,

'PS – Kyle has your eyes.'

And that was that. I never heard from her ever again.

Acknowledgements

I would like to thank the following people:

For inspiration: Dennis Potter, Nikos Kazantzakis, Arthur C. Clarke, William Peter Blatty, Charles Bukowski, Philip K Dick, John Fante, Christopher Marlowe, William Shakespeare and Johann Wolfgang von Goethe.

For help and support: David and Carol Armer, Amanda Webster, Anthony Peake, Alice Grist, John Hunt Publishing, the real Dave (hopefully living a better life in Hollywood, but probably not), my grandfather – Roland Watson – who died many years back but always believed in my talent – and last, but not least, I want to thank my beautiful daughter, Jessica Meredith Bryce Armer. Your father will always love you and always be proud of you. You are the absolute love of my life and my greatest inspiration.

I'd also like to mention all the negative people in my life who told me that it's wrong to dream and that I would amount to nothing. Well, we all return to dust at the end of the day, so the joke's on you. I hope the proud and bitter achievements in killing the dreams and aspirations of children served you well, O noble souls. I escaped you. And God give all children the strength and wit to avoid your bleak and angry pessimism, masquerading as wisdom.

Roundfire Books put simply, publish great stories. Whether it's literary or popular, a gentle tale or a pulsating thriller, the connecting theme in all Roundfire fiction titles is that once you pick them up you won't want to put them down.